# Confessions
# of a White Racist

## Also by Larry L. King

*Fiction*

The One-Eyed Man

*Nonfiction*

And Other Dirty Stories

# Larry L. King
# Confessions of a
# White Racist

## THE VIKING PRESS

New York

Copyright © 1969, 1971 by Larry L. King

First published in 1971 by The Viking Press, Inc.
625 Madison Avenue, New York, N.Y. 10022

Published simultaneously in Canada by
The Macmillan Company of Canada Limited

SBN 670-23715-9

Library of Congress catalog card number: 70-147391

Printed in U.S.A. by Vail-Ballou Press, Inc.

Parts of this book originally appeared in *Harper's Magazine* in somewhat
different form.

Acknowledgments: THE DIAL PRESS: from *Tell Me How Long the Train's
Been Gone* by James Baldwin. Copyright © 1968 by James Baldwin. JOHN-
SON PUBLISHING CO., INC.: from *Before the Mayflower: A History of Black
America* by Lerone Bennett, Jr. Copyright Johnson Publishing Company,
Inc., 1961, 1969. MCGRAW-HILL BOOK COMPANY: from *Soul on Ice* by
Eldridge Cleaver. Copyright © 1968 by Eldridge Cleaver. Used with
permission of McGraw-Hill Book Company. RANDOM HOUSE, INC.: from
*Eldridge Cleaver: Post-Prison Writings and Speeches,* edited by Robert
Scheer. Copyright © 1967, 1968, 1969 by Ramparts Magazine, Inc. From
*Invisible Man,* by Ralph Ellison. Copyright 1947, 1948, 1952 by Ralph
Ellison. Both reprinted by permission of Random House, Inc. WASHINGTON
POST AND ROGER WILKINS: for permission to reprint Mr. Wilkins' column;
© The Washington Post 1970. THE WORLD PUBLISHING COMPANY: from
*Miami & the Siege of Chicago* by Norman Mailer. Copyright © 1968 by
Norman Mailer. Reprinted by permission of The World Publishing Com-
pany.

For Rosemarie, again:
she truly understands

# Contents

Introduction ix

i: Whitey's Boyhood 1

ii: The Young Warrior 31

iii: Desert Transitions 59

iv: The Politician 97

v: On Through Mad Babylon 133

Epilogue 168

# Introduction

These introductory speeches usually begin with a polite curtsy and an attempt to define what one's book is. Let me spend small energies in bowing and tell quickly what mine is not.

It is not a book about black Americans so much as one about white Americans and their racist attitudes. It is not my individual confession alone, but a gratuitous admission of guilt on behalf of all white racists past and present, malignant or benign. It is not, I think (once the reader permits this opening oratory), a strident moral preachment so much as a journey of one white American who, boy and man, goes wandering through his time and his country. Sometimes he is blind; occasionally he sees. And always his journey is made easier by the color of his skin.

Few white Americans qualify as special authorities on the black man, his culture, or his history. I make no claims in that direction. Perhaps I have read a bit more on racial subjects, and have had the opportunity to observe white racism practiced at more varied social levels, in more geographic ports, and among more of our revered national institutions, than have the majority of white Americans. Consequently, I may have thought more on the subject of racism, and for longer, and with a touch more of caring in my heart. Maybe I have even come a longer way than most. This honor has its limitations (even presuming one is entitled to it) simply because the competition is of such poor quality.

Though our newspaper headlines and television screens have for almost twenty years shown daily evidence of a thousand dirty little domestic racial wars (and have revealed at least one racial injustice for every battle fought in those distressing if necessary conflicts), few white Americans seem willing to believe what their eyes or their ears or the Kerner Report clearly tell. Though black people comprise at least eleven per cent of our national population, rare is the white who may honestly claim a black as a personal friend—or even as a neighbor. I know whites from coast to coast who have neither entertained black people in their homes nor visited the homes of blacks. These sheltered many are not confined to the grubbier laboring classes or to gentle dowagers who teach piano in their parlors while recalling their heroic old Confederate grandaddies, but include doctors, lawyers, professors, colonels, editors, FBI agents, bankers, and members of Congress.

Let me not falsely represent myself as the pluperfect example of the white man who knows all, sees all, and understands everything about our black brothers and sisters. No, that particular strain of vanity among whites is too common to repeat here. A year never goes by, indeed, in which I cannot look back and see in my conduct or concepts some vestiges of white racism. Old poisons run deep.

I am perhaps best described as a white man, forty-two, a veteran observer of racist America, who has struggled for more than half his life to make some sense of the insanities of racial prejudice. This undertaking has been without success for the simple reason that no sanity resides therein. Like war, racial prejudice need not justify itself rationally in order to exist or even to thrive. All that is necessary for both war and racism to retain their high popularity are people who are willing to divide humanity into groups of "We" and "They" and then blithely to proceed as if "We" retain all exclusive solutions or traits.

Only so recently that it should bring blushes to our collective cheeks have we of America's majority race—we "Caucasians" —begun to think or to feel or even to understand marginally something of our long and sorry history as racists. Yet the sin is older than our nation. What is truly amazing is how many white Americans continue to deny their (and the nation's) unseeing or uncaring attitudes. Especially is this true of people of my age, or older. I don't know how much of this remarkable social myopia should be attributed to honest ignorance, how much deserves to be assigned to a decent sense of secret shame, or how much is accounted for by those ancient protective instincts which rouse themselves like barking dogs against the midnight footsteps of old dark fears installed by the myths, customs, and distortions of our past.

If today one could magically concoct a single white man and fairly charge him, as an individual, with all the racist crimes of America against one theoretical black man representative of his people's many victimizations, I am convinced, no jury in love with justice would have any recourse other than to hang him high, with the recommendation that he be permitted to strangle by fractions. To vote for Whitey's acquittal, our hypothetical jurors would find it necessary to ignore three hundred years of chicanery including kidnaping, slavery, broken family units and shattered promises, racial segregation with its debilitating humiliations accruing to the oppressor as well as to the oppressed, and, incredibly, murder by mob rule more than five thousand times within the first forty years of the twentieth century alone. Someone else must rise for the defense. I haven't any. This white man's burden is, simply, the white man's history.

The white American did not invent either slavery or racism. Archeological evidence suggests that man's earliest wandering tribes may have captured other humans for their handy uses. What we know of man's exploitative instincts down through recorded history suggests this possibility even more strongly. Slavery has existed to one degree or another in every nation, culture, or government known to man. There were slaves in the times of Moses, Plato, and Caesar. There were slaves in Africa before the white man arrived, and slaves in Europe long after it called itself Christian.

In the earlier times slaves were more often the booty of war. Conquerors simply appropriated the conquered as a matter of course. To win wars was to assure ample free labor for the Pyramids or Great Walls or other public works of the times, to say nothing of how handy slaves proved in the fields or around the house. While certainly many of these ancient wars did not go uninfluenced by racial differences or racist attitudes, slavery in the earlier time seems to have been a matter more of accident or luck than of pure racism. Any man could find himself a human chattel should he fight in one losing battle too many or be linked by citizenship with a nation's or a tribe's fallen cause.

It took the Christian Europeans to begin to make slavery a purely racial matter, and to refine its processes for steady profits—though the early Americans would eventually teach *them* a thing or two. Beginning in 1444, Europe enjoyed more than four centuries of brisk dealing in human flesh. Over forty million blacks are calculated to have been spirited away from Africa; uncounted millions died on stinking slave ships or during the brutal forced marches taking them down to the sea in chains.

The earliest French and Spanish expeditions to North America brought slaves. The first permanent settlement, a Spanish colony in what became South Carolina, included black slaves. There, in 1526, the first of more than two hundred and fifty slave revolts occurred in the New World—an awkward fact for those who contend that blacks have been happiest when in conditions of servitude, or were somehow willing to settle for less than first-class opportunities. It is uncertain how many of those first rebellious blacks survived: we do not know whether they were in time wholly assimilated by American Indians or were killed or died in short order.

Historians trace the American Negro's true beginnings to a later year, an August day in 1619 when a Dutch ship docked at Jamestown, Virginia, among settlers of the first English colony in the New World. Aboard were twenty blacks, captured on the high seas by the Dutch ship after it had done battle with a Spanish entry taking African migrants to the West Indies. The captain of the marauding Dutch vessel, manned by pirates who obviously had fallen on hard times in their trade, offered his human cargo in exchange for food supplies. The English settlers agreed. Five years later the first black baby was born to the English colony. The product of a union between two of the original blacks traded at Jamestown (young people recorded only as Anthony and Isabella) was christened William Tucker in honor of a white planter.

It is important to the purposes of history to remember that the twenty blacks who arrived in Jamestown in 1619 were not, strictly speaking, slaves. They were permitted to become "indentured servants," meaning that after a number of years in the service of whites (in repayment of the investments they represented) they would be permitted their freedom. In colonial times this was a common arrangement thought to accommodate poor whites, criminals, or adventuresome drifters who had left (or been expelled from) their European homelands. Though they passed to the highest bidder upon arrival in the New World, indentured servants could after five to ten years attain freedom. This practice existed for four decades during which many indentured servants—including a number of blacks— came to hold property, vote in local councils, enjoy general social acceptance, and even command their own temporary slaves. Racial intermarriages occurred; children were born of mixed unions both with and without the benefit of clergy.

Lerone Bennett, Jr., has written in his excellent *Before the Mayflower* of that crucial period when whites in the New World made the determination to enslave blacks, and why:

> The racial situation, at this juncture, was fluid; it contained the seed of several alternatives. Indentured servitude could have continued for black and white servants or both groups could have been reduced to slavery. Other possibilities were Indian slavery and a free labor system for blacks and whites, Indians and immigrants. Socio-economic forces selected Negro slavery out of these alternatives. In the West Indies, sugar was decisive. In America, tobacco and cotton were the villains. A world-wide demand for these products and the rise of plantation-sized units to meet this demand focused attention on the labor force. How could men be *forced* to work?

The rulers of the early American colonies were not overly scrupulous about the color or national origin of their work force. Indian slavery was tried and abandoned. Many masters attempted to enslave white men and white women. When these attempts failed, the spotlight fell on the African. He was tried and he was found not wanting. Why were Africans more acceptable than poor whites and poor Indians? White men, for one thing, were under the protection of strong governments; they could appeal to a monarch. White men, moreover, were white; they could escape and blend into the crowd. Indians, too, could escape; they knew the country, and their brothers were only a hill or a forest away. Another element in the failure of Indian slavery was the fact that Indians tended to sicken and die.

Africans did not have these disadvantages. They were strong: one Negro, the Spanish said, was worth four Indians. They were inexpensive: the same money that would buy an Irish or English indentured servant for ten years would buy an African for life. They were visible: they could run, but they could not blend into the crowd. Above all, they were unprotected. And the supply, unlike the supply of Irishmen and Englishmen, seemed to be inexhaustible. The rulers of early America fell to thinking. Why not?

Virginia and Maryland led the way in the 1660's. Laws made black men servants for life; intermarriage was forbidden; children born of African women were ruled bond or free, according to the status of the mother.

At first, religion was the rationalization. Negroes were good material for slavery because they were not Christians. Between 1667 and 1682, the basis shifted to race. Virginia said it first, in her law of 1667: ". . . the conferring of baptisme doth not alter the condition of a person as to his bondage or freedom." After that, it was easy. A series of laws stripped the Negro slaves of all rights of personality and made color a badge of servitude. The Negro population, which had grown slowly during the twilight interim of freedom, lunged forward. By 1710, the number had increased to 50,000. . . . By 1860 the twenty Negroes who landed at Jamestown in 1619 had become 4,000,000.

The shocking brutalities and specific debasements of American slavery have been many times documented in other books. Little reason, then, to replow that blood-sweat-and-tear-stained old ground here. Mine is largely a story of personal recollections of a much later time, of experiences in what we like to think of flatteringly as a more enlightened period. Suffice to say that in recalling American slavery we should remember that "peculiar institution" for the hard bitch she was, a mean old crone who killed, maimed, and wore out millions of black humans for profit and fun—and who twisted for generations to come the minds and souls of countless others, black and white. The old whore lived long and died fighting, leaving white racism as a legacy.

By 1883, only eighteen years after the Civil War had "freed" black people, our Supreme Court declared unconstitutional the Civil Rights Act of 1875 which had given blacks the right to equal treatment in hotels, places of public amusement, and public conveyances. The Court also ruled that the 14th Amendment to the Constitution merely prohibited states (as opposed to individuals) from discriminatory practices in the area of public accommodations. Thus was bigotry officially sanctioned by our highest tribunal; thus were Americans told in the most authoritative voices that it was permissible to treat some people differently from others because of their skin coloration.

The states, however, did not wait many years to demand the same prejudices granted to individuals. In 1890, Mississippi successfully disenfranchised its black voters by passing laws calling for "literacy and understanding tests," which were rigged against blacks in their application; most Southern states shortly followed Mississippi's lead. By 1900, virtually all national pretensions toward treating the Negro as an equal in matters of citizenship had vanished. Harsh Jim Crow laws had been passed throughout the South; in much of the nation Jim Crowism was efficiently practiced if not officially on the books.

In 1903, the Supreme Court verified which way the racial winds were blowing in upholding a test of Alabama's law disenfranchising black voters through "literacy" tests. A race riot in 1908 in Springfield, Illinois, led the following year to the founding of the National Association for the Advancement of Colored People. The Springfield riot was only the latest of twenty-five major race wars or massacres, dating from the Reconstruction period following the Civil War, in which at least four hundred blacks were murdered. These bloody statistics do not include "minor" incidents where whites lynched or shot individual Negroes, nor does it take into account many random burnings, bombings, or other harassments of black homes or gathering places.

In 1913, President Woodrow Wilson, that patrician Virginia gentleman and scholar who later would speak of fighting World War I in the name of a brotherhood of nations, permitted several of the larger federal bureaucracies to begin segregating federal employees by color. The Ku Klux Klan, reaching its peak strength in the 1920s both as a terrorist group and as a political power capable of including many elected officials in its ranks, was glorified and popularized in D. W. Griffith's film *Birth of a Nation*. Years later, my father would say that movie had played a large role in shaping his own racial attitudes and those of his contemporaries—just, I think, as the later misrepresentations of Amos 'n' Andy, Rochester, Stepin Fetchit, or 'Lasses and Honey greatly influenced my generation.

Though slavery had been officially banished from America for sixty-four years when I was born in Texas in 1929, white racism enjoyed a wide popularity: the 1920s were the most brutal of the modern decades in its lynchings or other mob actions against blacks. Economic boycotts began in 1929 in Chicago against white merchants who refused to hire Negroes, expanding to New York, Cleveland, and Los Angeles. A year later, the NAACP knew its first big success when it persuaded the United States Senate against confirming President Hoover's nominee to the Supreme Court, Judge John J. Parker of North Carolina, on the basis of his racist record.

Shortly after my second birthday, in 1931, the celebrated

trials of the Scottsboro Boys began in Alabama: nine black youths charged with raping two white doxies in a railroad boxcar. They were convicted and sentenced to death, on perjured testimony and some of the most dubious "evidence" ever presented to an American court. The resulting uproar may have marked the first time that a significant number of white Americans became exercised over the basic rights of black people, if we exclude the Abolitionists of slave days. In September of 1937, as I wrestled in a Texas schoolhouse with the thundering mysteries of the third grade, a black blues singer named Bessie Smith bled to death after a car wreck in Mississippi when all available medical attentions were directed toward whites injured in the same wreck. Marcus Garvey, a black nationalist who in the 1920s became the first effective organizer of the black masses (and whom James Baldwin credits with being the first to say "Black is beautiful") had long since been jailed by white America for mail fraud. A young black man named Adam Clayton Powell had led successful rent strikes in Harlem. Another named Richard Wright was writing an angry book called *Native Son*. In my youthful white world, I was oblivious to these events.

I don't think many writers sit at the typewriter with lying in mind, though perhaps by standard measurements we accomplish our share of it. Writers are dramatists by nature and requirement; they have been known to improve occasionally on the facts or the dialogue or the situation should improvements be convenient to their art. Writers have their vanities and egos to attend to the same as the rest of us, and so they generally cast themselves more nobly in print than they have conducted themselves on the stage of real events. Since we seldom see ourselves as others see us, even the writer hoping to establish new standards for honesty will be likely to gild his own lily with astounding consistency. Man's memory is not infallible; neither are his interpretations. Sometimes problems of story structure encourage the convoluting of time. Or the blurring of scenes or people becomes necessary. In short, pure unadulterated truth does not automatically leap from pen to page.

Because I think this book treats a vital subject, I have taken particular care to skirt these natural pitfalls. In drawing on conversations or experiences of which some are thirty-five years old, obviously I cannot certify all quotes as flawless. I have attempted, however, to re-create truly the dialogue, speech patterns, people, moods, and events here remembered; in no case have I altered the spirit, the basic circumstances, or the end results of my recollections. To do so would be to defeat my larger purpose of attempting accurately to reflect my time, my place, and my condition as it related to the most explosive social issue of my day.

For personal or legal reasons, I have attempted to disguise a few people and have failed to pinpoint a specific location or two. From experience, I know that some old friends, relatives, or associates will recognize themselves in so personal a recitation, no matter what beards I put them behind, and will be offended or hurt or both. This is particularly likely to be true of members of my immediate family, who are perhaps too clearly identified (and seemingly too summarily judged) to make either them or the author comfortable with the results. Some of the people I love most harbor their own disapproving opinions of my racial views, just as this book perhaps all too clearly reveals my disagreement with their attitudes. I hope they don't feel misused, but will consider themselves my companions in confronting important truths. My truths may not be theirs; truth is an elusive commodity, and each man must seek his own.

# i
# Whitey's Boyhood

"For all these years whites have been taught to believe the myth they preached, while Negroes have had to face the bitter reality of what America practiced. . . . It is remarkable how the system worked for so many years, how the majority of whites remained effectively unaware of any contradiction between their view of the world and that world itself. The mechanism by which this was rendered possible requires examination at this point."

—Eldridge Cleaver, *Soul on Ice*

**S**he was a big, dark, sorrowful woman, my Aunt Clara's domestic in a dusty little West Texas town—the first black person to register on my young mind. The New Deal was perhaps a year old, and I was five: a curious and excited farm boy reveling in his first extended town visit with its miracles of indoor plumbing, daily comic strips, and creamy fresh doughnuts brought home warm each night from my Uncle John's bakery.

I kept a safe distance in spying on the strange black creature while she dusted, made beds, swept, and mopped. Though my attentions were constant, we passed no words. I was introverted and shy; she seemed private, withdrawn, impervious to my stubborn scrutiny.

"Mama," I asked, "why is the ole nigger woman so sad?"

My mother recoiled with gentle murmurs of horror. "Oh, honey! Don't call her *that!* They want to be called colored folks. They get mad when you call 'em niggers." This warning, delivered in self-serving whispers, represents the only time I recall being chastised in my youth for racist reflexes.

The little Texas town where I was born discouraged Negro residents. I was fifteen before moving to a town where the black man was even statistically visible. On the June morning of 1937 following Joe Louis's knockout of Jimmy Braddock for the world heavyweight championship, I heard an old woman say in the Putnam post office, "Well, the ole nigger is champion." "Yes," her companion said. "I reckon they'll be pushing white folks off the sidewalks now."

The citizens of our town willingly fed most Depression hoboes who hopped off freights on the Texas & Pacific to beg food at our back doors, for we were of small-merchant Texas, dirt-farming Texas, Blood-of-the-Lamb Texas—not the oil-rich Texans of legend whom we suspected of impatience with failure and of a lukewarm Episcopalianism; we knew, therefore, something of empathy with the down-and-out. Our town knew, too, the loss of some of its own husbands or fathers or sons to the roads or to the rails in those cheerless times. When an infrequent black hobo appeared, however, our Good Samaritans were likely to drive him away with outraged oaths and threats to call the constable.

On our porch in the slow summer evenings where undistinguished dogs and small boys wondered at their inability to catch even one of a million darting fireflies, I often sat on my father's knee while he sang "The Nigger Preacher and the Bear" in a high, comic falsetto that never failed to please. The black preacher, out hunting quail and hare on the Sabbath against the natural laws of Heaven, is treed by an avenging bear. He is shot through with cowardice and malapropisms, and is so deserted by the presumably white God to whom he frantically prays that the bear is eventually permitted to squeeze the life from him—although, indeed, the black preacher gives a fair account of himself thanks to a congenital talent for expertly flourishing the razor. One of our family's private jokes, never told in the presence of company, concerned the horrifying moment when my older brother was discovered in the act of taking alternate bites off an apple with a Negro boy whose family paused briefly in Putnam. I remember the scandalized whispers when an eight-year-old cousin was caught playing bridegroom to a little black bride in a backyard mock wedding.

When I was perhaps eight or nine a touring minstrel show visited our town square, peddling vile patent medicines, sorry taffy candy with cheap treasures guaranteed in every box, and other useless gew-gaws. Shadows flickered and magnified themselves in the lights of kerosene lanterns brought by farm families or walking villagers to light their way to the cultural offering. The men wore faded denim overalls or patched khaki work pants, the collars of their tieless shirts carefully buttoned to identify them as gentlemen who knew better than to expose their undershirts or chest growths in mixed company. Their women I remember as stringy-haired and not normally of high humor, owners of sharp-pointed elbows, fierce creatures with some old granite of Pioneer Woman remaining in their faces. They all laughed as we laughed, however, at the foolish antics of Rastus and Sambo with their cork-blackened faces and exaggerated mouths grotesquely drawn in red cosmetics. The specific dialect jokes of those nights are lost in some old foggy 1930s memory bank, though I recall a bursting balloon sufficient to send the two scheming "darkeys" bolting in wall-eyed terror, while outsized fake feet on the actors assured continuous titters when the comic dialogue broke down.

For that matter, one would experience stereotyped "Negro humor" broadcast until recent years on the Amos 'n' Andy show (among others), the television version being no more sensitive to black feelings or culture than was the older radio version. Who does not readily recognize the white man's nigger as represented by the cast? Lawyer Calhoun pretended to a literacy so obviously impossible in a black man that he could only spout quasi-legalisms in the most unintelligible terms; Andy was a *cum laude* graduate of the School of Memorable Malapropisms as well as an inordinately sly dog among coveys of loose black ladies; "Lightnin' " from his office-boy station was so lazy he only reluctantly expended the energy required to breathe; George (Kingfish) Stevens embodied the sum qualities of all "bad niggers" everywhere—a con man who naturally preferred ill-gotten gains to honest labors, a philanderer even under the cold Black Maternalism eye of wife Sapphire, a circus nigger who dug parading in colorful lodge uniforms while pretending to ludicrous titles. Among regulars on the show only Amos was a good nigger, a white nigger, a nigger who might be trusted in the presence of the white man's money or his sister. He alone had a steady job or wanted one; he sometimes tried to persuade his black brothers to higher moral paths; he even paid his bills and told his children bedtime stories. Yes, Amos was what all his brothers might have become if only the black man had not been famed for excesses of larceny or so few brains.

For a period of thirty years this popular radio show may have burned the Negro stereotype into white minds more deeply than any other single mass-culture influence. "The only thing that's been more famous than Amos 'n' Andy," William Benton of the old Benton & Bowles advertising agency has said, "was Lindbergh's flight across the Atlantic." Benton persuaded Pepsodent to sponsor the show in the darkest Depression times; the company's sales quadrupled. When blacks mounted an effective protest against the television version in the late 1950s and early 1960s, some TV critics, a number of Congressmen, and several of my personal friends accused them of excessive sensitivity.

Quite without knowing how I came by the gift, and in a complete absence of even the slightest contact with black people, I assimilated certain absolutes: the Negro would steal anything lying around loose and a high percentage of all that was bolted down; you couldn't hurt him if you hit him on the head with a tire tool; he revered watermelon above all other fruits of the vine; he had a mule's determination not to work unless driven or led to it; he would screw a snake if somebody would hold its head.

Even our speech patterns were instructional: as we youngsters surreptitiously smoked cedar bark or dried grapevine in Cousin Kenneth's backyard storm cellar, we displayed generous contempt for the amateur who "nigger-lipped" the noxious offerings. To give participants in games of "Hide and Go Seek" time enough to conceal themselves, the hunter thrice or more intoned "Eenie meenie miney moe/Catch a nigger by the toe/If he hollers make him pay/Fifteen dollars every day." One's more menial labors could leave one "dirty as a nigger" or possibly "sweating like a nigger at election." Get a shade sunburned at the ole swimmin' hole, and your mother was sure to pronounce you "black as a nigger" even in the presence of your lobster-red qualities. Two objects instead of being as identical as "peas in a pod" were likely "as much alike as nigger soldiers." "I wouldn't feed it to a dog" was easily interchangeable with "It would choke a nigger." If you had an exceptional pal, you might boast that the two of you were "as close as runaway niggers." David may have slain Goliath with a slingshot, but in Putnam we warred on frogs, birds, and alley cats with "nigger-shooters." I don't remember that we employed our demeaning expressions in any remarkable spirit of vitriol: we were simply reciting certain of our cultural catechisms, and they came as naturally as breathing. For all of this, do not confuse my native ground with the lynching precincts of Mississippi, Georgia, or—even—East Texas. No, we were gentlemanly in our brutalities, even if only because we did not feel statistically threatened by blacks. Perhaps our racisms were more American than Confederate, in that I doubt whether—in the social and economic basics—we were significantly more discriminating than Evansville, Indiana; Dearborn, Michigan; or such stops as Kansas and Maine.

When we abandoned Putnam for our losing struggles against a series of neglected old farms in adjoining Eastland County, we found it unnecessary to adjust our speech habits or attitudes. Each time Joe Louis fought, the farmers of our community and their sons gathered before a common old battery-operated radio in the unifying prayer that some "white hope" would whip ole Joe's black ass for us. When Louis consistently rendered senseless our best fistic heros, we suspected that his opponents had been drugged or ordered by Chicago gangsters to take a dive. Despite the earlier examples of Jack Johnson or Joe Gans, we could not imagine a black man conquering a white man in the absence of chicanery.*

On alternate Saturdays I accompanied my father to Cisco, bumping eight miles over graveled roads in a horse-drawn flat-bed wagon. These were trips approached in the spirit of high adventure, for Cisco was a bustling entry of some six thousand; a boy lucky enough to own nine cents might find himself wit-

---

* Years later, reading *The Autobiography of Malcolm X* and Maya Angelou's *I Know Why the Caged Bird Sings,* I would learn that blacks gathered around their radios to root Joe Louis home for the same tribal reasons for which we whites assembled to hopefully await his defeat.

nessing Tom Mix or Buck Jones in their satisfying conquests of the savage Redmen, or observing Tarzan in his paternalistic supervision of apes and black Africans who looked on him as their natural leader. We tied the horses under an old mesquite tree behind a decrepit cotton gin before going off for grocery staples impossible to till in our fields, for the luxury of a fifteen-cent haircut, or on other errands of commerce. Here, on the wrong side of the tracks, where poor whites and Negroes jointly fulfilled their small commercial possibilities, one began to notice that black citizens somehow appeared "different."

Though poverty was a condition with which I early became familiar, nobody seemed quite as poor as the blacks. Their clothing was older than ours, ill-fitting almost always, sometimes held together by strings, wires, or possibly miracles of the will. The men, especially, shuffled along as if ravaged by old age or rheumatism, careful to nod and smile tentatively at my father should they meet in close quarters on unpaved stretches of South Cisco streets. I do not recall that he often returned their timid greetings. Sometimes I wondered if he saw them—though I was somehow afraid to ask. In retrospect, I think the rules probably required my father to take notice of black men only if they *failed* to be obsequious. In the seedy barber shop where I reported for infrequent store-bought haircuts, the aging black shoeshine "boy" was quick to grin or laugh when his white superiors made him the target of their rough country humor. And in McGlassen's Grocery, black men or women stepped back to permit white customers easy access to the vegetable bins or to the single check-out counter. I accepted this as being of the natural order.

With the outbreak of World War II, unusual job opportunities awaited middle-aged white men such as my father despite their lack of education or modern skills. The prospect of a weekly pay check almost tempted the King family to cheer the treachery of the Japanese. The best offer came in mid-1942 from a New Mexico outpost of the El Paso Natural Gas Company: if only we would move the necessary three hundred miles or so westward, my father would be paid seventy-eight cents per hour merely for lifting the heaviest objects the company produced in its Pipeline Division. This exceptional deal was approached with caution, however, for at thirteen I was presumed to be at an impressionable age—and the little New Mexico town was said to tolerate open saloons and niggers in its schools.

Only the former of these rumored degradations proved true when we reached Jal, a tiny hamlet in the southeastern corner of New Mexico, situated among dirty-tan sandhills only a dozen miles across the comforting Texas border. I once spotted a black couple and their two teen-age daughters in Tony Hurta's grocery; somebody said the black family worked for a rancher in the lonesome territory. Nobody knew, however, where the girls went to school . . . or even whether they did. On another occasion I was enjoying a cold soda-pop at Houston Wink's Service Station when a black man driving a big car bearing California license plates had the misfortune to stop for gasoline in that instant when our local deputy sheriff happened by. The lawman searched the car for mysterious contraband and required the traveler's life story before permitting him to proceed.

One afternoon, as we Jal Panthers practiced football, two black soldiers appeared among the local barber-shop loafers and pool-hall refugees who routinely abandoned their daily stations to observe the young knocking heads. One of our school officials approached the black soldiers to inquire whether he might help them. No, they had been passing by on the highway, had observed our football scrimmage in progress, and had a little time on their hands. "Well, I tell you," the school man said, "we don't like to practice in front of strangers. You see, we don't hold open workouts before a big game. I'll have to ask you to leave." We young football heroes did not always desire such fierce protection from inferior races: the night a half dozen of us witnessed our first Lena Horne movie we affirmed without a dissenting adolescent voice that there was one nigger we'd purely love to fuck.

In the middle of World War II we returned to Texas, moving to Midland in the oil-laden Permian Basin. Midland looked both east and west for its influences, three hundred miles in each direction. Dallas, to the east, provided an example in its pretentious homes, aggressive boosterisms, and select ruling oligarchy. We shared with westernmost El Paso an arid landscape not much different from the moon's as lately we have come to know it, along with that general unrest indigenous to a people beset over the years by Spanish *conquistadores,* marauding Indians, and those eternal gritty sands shifting and blowing in oven temperatures. Though Midland claimed a disproportionate share of wealth for an isolated village of twelve thousand (satisfying fortunes had been established in cotton and cattle before soil erosion, oil gushers, and mini-skyscrapers then reaching twelve stories high had transformed the lonesome prairie from agrarian to industrial), my father signed on as an oil-company night watchman for little more than a dollar an hour.

Midland had its "old" pioneer aristocracy; if their pedigrees were inferior to those held by the Cabots or the Lodges they didn't let on. A secondary social formation was comprised of the cream of the awakening oil industry. The perceptive, however, must have discerned that genealogy was prized far beyond the accidents of geology—especially if the genealogy contained an affluent mix. While the district manager of an oil company, even though recently removed from New Jersey or Tulsa, might soon become a power among Rotarians or at the country club, he should never assume his sons would automatically be welcomed to certain root celebrations.

The son of the night watchman, the railway clerk, or the town cop (if unusually handsome, exceptionally gifted at athletics, or of stunning scholastic prominence) might be invited to a few parties by New Money sources feeling out their social way. He might even be asked on special occasions (graduation night, for example, or when one of our first-family belles announced her engagement to his fellow co-captain of the basketball squad) to visit some of the old homes. He would go there in boilings of ecstasy and fear, conscious that his three-year-old suit did not always cover as much of his wrists or ankle bones as the factory had originally intended; afraid that exotic dishes might be served in a moment when he had no notion whether they should be attacked with knife, fork, spoon, or any combination thereof; wary of modern mothers who drank and danced; envious of the assured black men who padded in and out regally bearing trays of goodies. He might have a quick fantasy or two, involving a romance with one of the first-family belles in his own right, triggered by nothing more than a smile or backclap from the town's leading banker or cattle baron. He would also have ample opportunities, however, to ponder why he had been overlooked when invitations went out to other festivities on Country Club Circle, Brunson Avenue, or West Missouri Street.

The son of a certain night watchman did not then suspect half as much as he now understands of inherited limitations, and so he hopefully drove himself to performances beyond his normal athletic capacities as well as to the district debate championship, class offices, roles in amateur theatricals, and work on the school newspaper and yearbook. Such "accomplishments" primarily signify the youth's pathetic thirst for some vague assimilation or acceptance.

Because domestic jobs as cooks, maids, butlers, and gardeners were always available in the affluent homes of Midland, the little city's black population was larger and more visible, in the daylight hours anyway, than I had known before. At sundown black women waited in the alleys behind their places of employment for their husbands or sons to fetch them in one quaking old smoke-belching car or another. Then they would rattle off down East 80 past our central business district, the rodeo arena, tin-topped garages advertising mechanics on duty (the "N" in "Mechanics" quite often reversed, or the word perhaps inventively ending in an "X"), past a Mexican restaurant or two, and on by the Blue Goose Tavern before going south across the railroad tracks to their shacks or tents, barbecue stands, storefront prayer halls, and beer joints in the lowlands ghetto known as "the Flats."

Rain did not often water desert West Texas, but when it did one could count on the Flats' rapidly flooding. Not until years later would I appreciate the true poverty of the Flats: no paving for roadbed or sidewalks, no curb drainage, no hospital, no fire station or substation, no newspaper, no bank, no clothing store, no movie house, no lawyer's office, no Post Office substation, no Piggly-Wiggly or Woolworth's outlet—not even a gas station. Never would it have crossed my vacant mind that blacks might someday attend schools north of the railroad tracks, or even that they might wish to. I did not dwell on either the efficiency or the social necessity of having "White" and "Colored" waiting rooms in our tiny train depot with its limited traffic, any more than I lost sleep over blacks being arbitrarily herded to balcony seats should they choose to visit the Yucca or Texas theaters. I was equally oblivious to those nuances of justice or custom requiring blacks to move to the rear of the rattling old buses operated by our local City Lines. Those common little signs of some glittering substance mounted on colorful cardboard, and advertising that particular chili parlors or bowling alleys Reserve the Right to Refuse Service to Anyone, inspired no more reflections than did those signs intended to enlist me in the cause of Dr. Pepper or Mrs. Baird's Bread.

Our town policemen diligently patrolled the Flats to discourage whites from "being down here after dark." A single carload of white teen-agers in search of beer or general mischief was certain to be stopped by cops warning, "These niggers don't bother us at night and we ain't gonna let you bother them. You boys go home some night with the clap or get rolled down here, and we never *will* hear the last of it from your mammas and daddies."

We Midland High School Bulldogs played our well-attended

football games on Friday nights; the George Washington Carver Hornets played on what we considered "our field" on Thursday or Saturday nights as it became available. Although our fifty-yard-line tickets went for all of a dollar-six-bits, you could watch the Hornets from the better seats for fifty cents. We sometimes visited Carver games, swaggering in our purple and gold letter jackets, sure of our superiority as men and athletes. We laughed at the high-stepping antics of the Carver band ("They move in jig time," we cracked) and selected the strutting drum majorette most likely to assist in "changing our luck." We were disappointed when the stands failed to erupt into multiple razor fights, as we had every confidence they would.

After one Carver victory we were leaving the stadium, loud and boisterous in the exhilarations of youth, when we passed the Carver football bus loading for its return to the dusty Flats. A big Carver lineman called from the bus, "Hey, Bulldogs, yawl think yawl can play football?" We stood rooted, amazed at his black audacity. "Bet we can beat you," he said. "Yawl get all the newspaper headlines, but we got the team. *Everybody* know a Hornet can sting a ole Bulldog." The Carver lads laughed and hooted. "Ask your coach to scrimmage against us sometime," another voice called from inside the bus. "Unless yawl are fraidy-cats."

We stood mute as the bus pulled away, though Burton, a wild and wiry little wingback, recovered sufficiently to shout, "Piss on you, you boog fuckers"—for which withering witticism we young gentlemen roundly congratulated him. Over cherry Cokes and hamburgers at the Minute Inn we boasted of how we would stomp those black bastards 60 to 0 if only our authorities would permit.

One might have thought we had proposed naked dancing girls serving free beer in study hall. No sir, a school official said (his mouth puckering as if he had just sampled an alum milkshake), it just wouldn't be done! One of our coaches barked, "We got our hands full playing Abilene and San Angelo back-to-back. I hear any more about this Carver crap, and there'll be enough extra wind sprints to keep air and ideas off your brains." Word somehow got around that I had originated the idea of "playing the niggers." Aldrich, from one of our better families and rumored to be powerful in the semisecret and ultra-snobbish High-Hatters Society functioning on campus, accommodated me in a fistfight behind the gym by way of straightening out my role. The young lady who most consistently cavorted through my sexual fantasies refused to go out with me again.

In our classrooms they told us of Booker T. Washington, who, like Joe Louis, had proved "a credit to his race"—the clear implication being that Mr. Washington was an exceptional creature, something of a congenital freak from among an inferior species. George Washington Carver may have been named in passing, and possibly Carter G. Woodsen was, though five minutes later we probably couldn't have related their special accomplishments. A. Phillip Randolph's name was never revealed, since he had socialistic twitches and was connected with the plots of labor unions. Nobody revealed the many anguished and outraged utterances of Frederick Douglass, the former slave who once remarked, "Slaves are expected to sing as well as work"; nor did they report on his Boston speech of 1849: "I should welcome the intelligence tomorrow, should it come, that slaves had risen in the South, and that the Sable arms which had been engaged in beautifying and adorning the South were engaged in spreading death and devastation." There was no accounting of such black artists as the internationally celebrated Colonial poetess Phyllis Wheatley, or of Langston Hughes, Arna Bontemps, Richard Wright, Paul Robeson, James Weldon Johnson. Although *Uncle Tom's Cabin* was never on our required reading lists, our American history class was marched to the Yucca Theater to be educated by *Gone with the Wind*; I do not recall that Rhett Butler, Scarlett O'Hara, or Butterfly McQueen did or said anything to alter our racial misunderstandings. We heard nothing at all of such black deviationists or revolutionaries as W.E.B. DuBois, Marcus Garvey, Nat Turner, David Walker, Gabriel Prosser, Denmark Versay. Crispus Attucks came in for minor mention as having been the first man to die in the American Revolution, though the text made it clear he may have blundered into a stray bullet during the Boston Massacre. As we were not told that Paul Revere had alerted blacks as well as whites to menaces posed by the oncoming British, we had no way of knowing that some five thousand black American Revolutionaries took up arms against the oppressions of a wicked king; thus was it made to appear that Crispus Attucks' sacrifice, whether intentional or accidental, might have been as exceptional as Booker T. Washington's intellect or Joe Louis's fists.

Possibly it is just as well that our professors failed to disturb the deep sleep of history. Otherwise, a generation of schoolboys might have learned that General George Washington originally did not trust blacks for chores of combat, or (jumping a few wars ahead) that even after President Lincoln signed the Emancipation Proclamation he not only ordered that black troops be segregated but also decreed their pay to be lower than that of their white contemporaries. And though we suffered the required study of Texas history down to the lamentable death of the last heroic defender of the Alamo against alien Mexican hordes, and once enjoyed a class outing to the ruins of Old Fort Davis (a frontier military post advertised as having been created to protect West Texas "pioneers" from the savage Indian and to assure passage of the United States mails between San Antonio and El Paso), no one troubled to say that the old fort's protective duties had been performed almost exclusively by black troops feared by the Indians for their efficient fighting qualities. And who told us of the black cowboys helping to tame those Western frontiers to which we pledged allegiance from our desert latitudes?

As for the "peculiar institution" that was slavery (our lessons ran), well, perhaps slavery *was* slightly awkward in its arrangements when considered in hindsight or against values propagandized in the frigid, meddling North—though probably most slaves had had it cushier than black "freedmen" ill-equipped through nature and training to handle the multiple responsibilities of freedom. And, besides, there had been all that tobacco to harvest and cotton to pick in the name of Bringing Forth on This Continent a New Nation Conceived in Liberty, etc. Once past the temporary embarrassment of human bondage, our teachers plunged with ill-concealed relief into what a dark Reconstruction we in the misunderstood South had suffered, what with all those looting Billy Yanks, profiteering Carpetbaggers, and sullen black "freedmen" blighting land intended for us by God and Jefferson Davis. Probably even then the most shiftless of these were plotting to get themselves on the welfare roles.

Among the best-kept secrets of Midland High School were those accrued to the white race when our slave ships, making their first journeys from Africa in the early seventeenth century, provided death to thousands through their cramped quarters, lack of sanitary facilities, chains, and whips. No one told us that black people died in their own excrement, crazed by fevers and fear, packed together in a breathless mass sucking life and hope. Nor were we advised that black "savages" from the jungles had developed a religious belief of life in the Hereafter —even in the absence of Methodist missionaries—so that many jumped to their watery deaths rather than face a life in bondage. Nobody instructed us that in order to discourage slave rebellions the white peddlers of black flesh systematically broke up family or tribal units so that easy communication among surviving blacks would be impossible due to their diverse languages, values, and cultures.

I was a grown man before discovering that George Washington and Thomas Jefferson (those wise, saintly men whose pronouncements on liberty and justice leaped from my textbooks and echoed from the mouths of our Independence Day orators, those Forefathers whose wartless and inspiring faces looked down from their places of honor on our classroom walls) had owned slaves. It was shocking to learn that demigods who had influenced documents affirming the thrilling, limitless doctrine that *all men are created equal* had been otherwise capable of holding men in bondage for the profit from their sweat. I well remember discovering these new lessons in the Midland County Library, in my twenty-first year, and then standing outside, looking up at the windswept streets, and thinking, "Hell, if they lied to me about *that,* they've lied to me about everything." Only independent adult research would ultimately alert me that some of New England's proudest old families had dealt in slaves, that black flesh was peddled on the Boston Common, or that a few years before black slaves came in chains New Englanders impatient for help at less than prevailing wage rates had enslaved a few stray Indians. Our school textbooks preached that most slaveholders had been kindly to their chattels more often than not, selling a father away from his wife and children only when absolutely necessary and always with the greatest personal regret. Nor did our textbooks stress that Mr. Lincoln and his Abolitionist friends became more than marginally concerned with the slave's plight only after the time had safely passed when the black man was absolutely vital to Northern crop-gathering, and was neither particularly desired for, nor thought capable of, participation in the new industrialization. Nowhere, in my early association with our educational or other institutions, was it hinted that black people had played sustaining roles in our national history or had made significant contributions to American culture.

In 1944 the Supreme Court declared unconstitutional the Texas "white man's primary"—a dodge by which the Democratic Party in some areas precluded blacks from voting by limiting participation to "Caucasians," and which the Republicans surely would have copied had they had enough votes in those days to trouble with primary elections. This decision caused great consternation in east Texas (I would later learn), where the black population posed a presumed statistical threat to customs and habits of Democracy. Perhaps the elders of my West Texas village were also distraught, regardless of their overwhelming superiority in numbers over blacks, though probably I would not have taken the smallest notice of the Supreme Court's decision had not one of our teachers invited in a local politician to rant against Washington for so foully intruding in processes better left to hometown hearts. Never did I hear it suggested from podium or pulpit that perhaps the black citizen had a rawer deal than our Constitution recommended. Perhaps no label was applied, but certainly we were more than accidentally encouraged to believe in the Manifest Destiny of the superior white race.

Some of the more obvious white-supremacy advocates of my youth were men of the cloth. My father was himself a sometime country preacher without the benefit of formal training or official sanction, though he had in his sixteenth year quite clearly heard the Call while working one hot day in a cornfield. Our home in my formative years was fair game for a series of trembling itinerant prophets who, upon completing a wild pulpit-pounding sermon only thirty minutes shorter than the Fundamentalist concept of Eternity's promises or threats, descended to gobble up the best pieces of my mother's fried-chicken dinners. Though the chicken-eating talents of those visiting preachers distressed me from palate to gizzard, they were perhaps not half so painful as the endless, boring afternoons to follow: boys from Fundamentalist homes were allowed only accidental Sabbath joys on the theory that noise, play, or the slightest titillation might disturb our stern God in His restful meditations. Since I had nothing more exciting to do than monitor the chatter of grown-ups, my education was furthered: I recall convincing dissertations on how the earth was most assuredly flat, the Scriptures speaking of winds "blowing from the four corners of the earth"; I heard enough of the Virgin Birth to account for everything but its biological specifics.

One of the favored topics of those unlettered priests was the vast amount of Scriptural authority accounting for the black man's lowly state and substandard conduct. Ham had taken a wife from among a tribe marked by the curse of Cain—some low-rated beast of the field she was, probably little better than a first cousin to the gorilla. From this unnatural union (so ran the prevailing theology) had been produced the most primitive form of the black race. God's all-seeing eye had been so displeased that His book forever consigned blacks to be "hewers of wood and drawers of water," "a servant's servant" happiest when waiting tables, playing banjo, or riding in the back of the bus.

The ministers of my teen-age experiences were sometimes smoother in their presentations, and some may have harbored slightly more modern attitudes: my father held them in contempt because they "preached from notes" instead of letting the spontaneous Word of God flow through them as human transmitters the way Heaven had originally intended. Even one of our more sophisticated ministers, however, was privately known for possibly the largest repertoire of "nigger jokes" in all the Sixteenth Congressional District. A preacher from a smaller sect brought around the coach from his denomination's church-supported college in my junior year to sound me out about a possible football scholarship. Thanks, I mumbled, but I hoped to attend a Big School somewhere—had even considered going off to a City School in the North if that miracle might somehow be arranged. Better I should have declared a preference for the pagan idols and heathen teachings of Notre Dame. The shocked Fundamentalist missionary demanded to know why. Well, I said, I wanted to see other parts of the country— was curious to experience life outside the sandy horse-latitudes of my birth. Whereupon the minister shed a mid-week sermon: *Well, now, boy, you go way off up yonder to play ball and you gonna run into lots of strange thangs—sin in its most venal forms, uncommon manners, crazy ideas.*

Possibly the anticipatory gleam in my eyes alerted the preacher's professional parts that here was a young man hopelessly enamored of sin-in-the aggregate, and so he became more threateningly specific: *Why, son, up there in the North they gonna make you play ball with niggers and maybe feed you and sleep you with 'em and use the same drinking fountains, and when it's all over ain't nobody up there gonna give a hoot about you and you'll have to hurry on home. And folks down here, now, they good people and all that; they take care of their own. Business people, now, they not gonna have much confidence in a fellow who's been off up yonder four years where so many strange ideas have taken a-holt. I just think you'd be making a terrible mistake to mark yourself in the community that-a-way. You come on down to little ole So-and-So College, now, and we gonna make you into a good Christian left tackle the community will be proud to welcome back.*

Nor were our newspapers any more instructional than our preachers or teachers. They were strong for "states' rights," not even admitting to the possibility of state wrongs, either on their editorial pages or by vigorous investigative reporting. Our editorials were full of enough Boosterisms to have gladdened the blood of George Babbitt. While community customs encouraged gross social inequities, our editorial writers were content to welcome visiting Lions Clubs or to praise the Chamber of Commerce for its industry-attracting programs whenever a bootmaker opened a new shop or a major oil company moved in a few more white-collar employees. Once monthly, when local banks reported their deposits, our newspaper's banner headline could be counted on to brag of record prosperity. There were enthusiastic front-page blurbs on alternate Mondays for $DOLLAR DAYS$ with their unmatched bargains for lucky shoppers, and an immense preoccupation with growth for growth's sake; one almost pitied those clods unfortunate enough to be stuck in Manhattan, San Francisco, or London. Still, though the newspaper backed the Chamber of Commerce in advertising our town as "Ever-Growing Midland," "Smiling Midland" and "Magnificent Midland," the world ignored our billing.

When the League of United Latin American Citizens attacked our perfect town for its alleged discrimination against citizens of Mexican descent, pointing to their outdoor privies

and second-hand opportunities, our paper published an outraged editorial naming Midland the very essence of a pure Democracy. Our newspaper had no black or Mexican editors or
reporters, of course, nor any black or Mexican linotype operators, advertising salesmen, or secretaries, and not even one
black newsboy. I think, however, that I remember a black or a
Mexican or two among the janitorial corps.

When I was sixteen I worked out of the Midland post office
as a mailman. My route that summer went to many of our leading homes, some few of which I had violated socially. Frequently a carload of my more privileged contemporaries zipped
by on wisps of gasoline, perfume, or beer, the occupants calling
back greetings lost on the wind as they headed for a dip in the
country-club pool or to the Turners' tennis courts or to the
Cowdens' for a patio cookout. The night watchman's son
plodded along under a fiery desert sun and the burden of a
mailbag, cursing his birthright while indulging in brain-movies
about his return to Midland in later years to receive the town's
congratulations on the books he had written, the medals he had
won at war, and the Hollywood hearts he had broken for reasons of mischief or whimsy.

One afternoon in the post office I found my fellow letter carriers in a private huddle. Slim, a big-boned redneck in his thir-
ties, spoke for the older carriers to the three of us working as
the summer vacation help. "The postmaster is hirin' a nigger,"
he said. "He says one of us got to take the nigger around our
route and train him. Well, *I* ain't gonna. And Red ain't and
Don ain't and Cecil ain't. They'll probably try to push the jig
off on one of you kids. If you let 'em get away with it, we
won't have nothing but nigger carriers in six months." A few
minutes later I was called to the postmaster's office.

Postmaster Noel G. Oates was a friendly, easy man who han-
dled his job in a low key, a former walking mailman who knew
the hazards of dog bite and thirst. On that summer afternoon so
long ago, however, I would learn that he contained a certain

steel. He began by telling of his difficulty because of the war-time manpower shortage, then said he had hired a young Negro just returned from the military. "I've decided you would be the best man to train him," he said.

"No," I said. "I can't do it."

Possibly the postmaster sat a bit straighter in his chair: "Why?"

"Well, none of us wants to do it. We've been talking about it."

"Give me your reasons for not wanting to."

"Well, hell . . . he's a *nigger*. And all the other guys will be mad if I do it. And I don't want everybody from school seeing me work with him."

"We're not gonna debate it," Mr. Oates said. "I've got my job to do, and if you can't do yours you can turn in your time. You've got until eight o'clock tomorrow morning to make up your mind."

I first consulted with my teen-age contemporaries on the summer gig, Tabor and Davis, who delighted in making clear it was not their problem and then went happily off to the roller rink. I then sought out my father, who said it was the kind of decision each man must make for himself. He sat on a carpenter's sawhorse in the backyard, whittling with his pocket knife, his lower lip bulging with Garrett's Snuff: he understood how I felt; on the other hand, I did need the job. So work it out in my own mind. Pray on it.

The following morning, as I sorted the mail for delivery, Postmaster Oates appeared with Tim—a dark young man in his early twenties, neat and tense. We shook hands (the first time I had suffered such an intimacy with a black man); after a few joshing words meant to ease the strain, the postmaster left us. I explained the mail-sorting processes to Tim, painfully aware of the malevolent glances the sullen Slim cast, and of the snickers and whispers of Red and Don. (Cecil had turned in his time, on the theory that his own turn at "nursemaiding niggers" was then being planned in secret councils, to become a rack boy in a pool hall—where, ironically, he worked side by side with two black rack boys). When the rest of us adjourned to Agnes's Café for lunch, Tim ate from a brown bag under a tree at the rear of the post office.

Tim shared my route for two weeks. Though we were carefully polite, we had no conversations beyond the job at hand or routine agreements on the weather. Several times I was embarrassed when we encountered my classmates while walking in affluent neighborhoods; good ole Slim could always be depended on at the end of each work day to grant me an exaggerated mock inspection meant to determine "how much of the black is rubbin' off." The day Tim was assigned his own route was a happy one for me. Other carriers, however, complained that Tim had been assigned a convenient downtown route coveted by older heads whose letter-carrying led them to the edges of limitless desert spaces, through dog territory, and deep into bunion country. Complaints decreased when a supervisor explained front-office logic: "Well, you see, we'll have less fussing from merchants than we would from private householders. I mean, nobody cares if a Nigra comes in their store, but suppose he brings a postage-due letter to somebody's house when the wife is alone and in her slip. . . ."

The summer of 1946 began in the oil fields (where, not so incidentally, I never saw a single black man employed among the thousands who flocked in to enjoy our booming prosperity, any more than I observed black men or women among the white-collar workers who emptied the downtown office buildings of our major oil companies at five p.m. each day). We lowly roustabouts piss-anted heavy joints of pipe, and dug pits and ditches. One stifling July afternoon I emerged from cleaning an oil-storage tank, sweating and reeking of Waste of Petroleum, when it occurred to me that no law in the world said I ever had to clean another. I was completing my third or fourth hitch in the oil patch (having lied shortly before my fourteenth birthday to obtain a job in a clean-up crew) and such romance as had attended working around hard-drinking, hard-swearing older men had long since faded despite adventures at poker tables, in beer joints, or in tin-topped hotels where girls were frequently rented. Within an hour I had drawn my time.

This impulsive act forced an agonized decision: whether to remain in school or join the Army. I was to have graduated two months earlier, in May, but had permitted coaches, school officials, and businessmen hyperactive in the Bulldog Booster Club to persuade me that I should deliberately fall one credit short of my diploma so I could again serve Midland High on the football field. (This "laying over," as it was called, was then a common schoolboy practice among athletes, though it has long since been outlawed.) They made flattering predictions: "Why, a big old tough boy like you could make All-State. Then all the big Southwest Conference colleges would line up to offer you scholarships." The Midland Bulldogs competed in a schoolboy super league which in that era sent such talents as Bobby Layne, Doak Walker, Kyle Rote, and Buddy Howton to spectacular collegiate careers at the University of Texas, SMU, and Rice, before forwarding them to glory in the National Football League. Faced with impossible dreams made to sound easy, I was rapidly convinced that the bells of fame might next toll for me.

I came to regret the scheme shortly after agreeing to it. Another year of high-school tedium, with its drowsy study halls and its torturous algebra classes where Miss McGee's curiosity about how much $x$ might currently equal seemed insatiable, suddenly loomed as pointless and unbearable; I was anxious to seek a larger world. Drake and I had, indeed, sought out the local Navy recruiter just as the school term ended (selecting the Navy over other military units because it was said to admit fewer blacks) but I failed the physical because of faulty depth perception. On the basis of a preliminary eye test, an Army recruiter had virtually guaranteed my acceptance and promised I could attain my lacking credit for graduation by passing a High School Equivalency Test. On quitting the oil patch I persuaded my parents to sign consenting papers, using as my clincher the argument that upon discharge I would be eligible for collegiate refurbishing under the GI Bill of Rights. The Army awarded thirty days in which to close out what it grandly referred to as my "civilian affairs."

I first hitchhiked to Amarillo, arriving in the back of a pickup truck on the tops of coops of squawking chickens, where I blew half my $180 bankroll buying bootleg whiskey for two aging prostitutes who delighted my hotel room between the profitable appointments to which they were summoned by a black bellhop. A drunk Indian in an Oklahoma City beer joint guzzled and conned his way through much of my remaining resources on some blowsy promise to introduce a beautiful tribal princess, to whom he gave the qualities of Hedy Lamarr in heat and loincloth. One purposeless morning, while touring for fifty cents an old farm house said to have been the hideout of the outlaw Dalton Brothers near Dodge City, Kansas, I impulsively opted to return to Putnam, the little town of my birth, for what I dramatically assumed would be my last inspection. A couple of days later, a bit road-grimy, I arrived near sundown in the Texas village of Albany. Of my remaining seven dollars, I invested two in a decrepit hotel room.

The bellhop was a fat, middle-aged Negro with drooping eyelids; though I had only a small canvas bag he insisted on taking it to my room. He opened the steamy room's single window, drew a pitcher of tepid tap water, and made other busywork motions. "Young mister," he said, "you like to buy a little pussy?"

Well, maybe. How much was it?

"You work that out with the girl. You ever changed your luck?"

Though I knew full well what he meant I blurted, "What?"

"Colored nookie. You ever had you any colored nookie?"

Well, no.

"You got anything against it?"

Well. No. Not really.

"She be here in a half hour," he promised, then extracted one of my disappearing dollars as his service charge.

I think I began the transaction as a lark. Certainly I was mindful of my destitute condition while almost two hundred miles from home, though by the time I heard the lady's knock my enthusiasm was genuine. Possibly this was because I had convinced myself she would be a ringer for Lena Horne, down to her very light, very bare skin. I was startled when she proved bony, darker than bittersweet chocolate, and wildly frizzy-haired. She was perhaps seven years my senior, perhaps ten; she wore a sagging skirt and a thin blouse denying even the promise of breasts.

"Well," I said by way of openers, "how much?"

"Ten dollar straight and fifteen dollar for French," she mumbled.

"Well, I'll give you three dollars for a straight date."

"Shit! Eight, or we can't do no business."

"I ain't got that much."

"How much you got?"

"Four," I admitted. "And maybe a little change."

"Goddamn you," she flared. "And here I went and dressed and owe a man a goddamn taxi fare! You white asses come over here from Breckenridge and Abilene and Cisco looking to get your jassam free. I got two little babies to feed."

"Oh," I said, inanely. "I didn't know you were married."

"Kiss my dead ass," the disgusted young woman said, slamming the door.

I thought about it, loosely concluding that when a nigger wench dared issue such vulgar invitations to a young white gentlemen, difficult times lay ahead.

My civilian affairs satisfactorily in order and my money gone, I reached Midland some three or four days ahead of my scheduled shipment to military control. I spent the remaining free time making the rounds of local teen-age hangouts, digging the diverse talents of Ernest Tubb, June Christie, and Glenn Miller in a time when juke-box songs sold for a nickel each or six for a quarter. At the slightest opportunity I hinted to young bobby-soxers that some dangerous, if highly classified, military mission awaited my special warrior's skills. The hope here was that my uncertain future might encourage intimate farewells, though possibly my act might have been more persuasive had not word been carelessly circulated that World War II's fighting phase had been concluded almost a year earlier.

On the night before my departure by bus for initial processing at Goodfellow Field near San Angelo, my friend and fellow Bulldog, Burton, accompanied me on visits to several beer joints where management generously overestimated young customers' ages should they be able to walk without accidents and wish to invest their money wisely. Late in the evening we called on Midland's one "black and tan" joint, an unpainted hovel on that subtle line where Niggertown and Meskintown uneasily joined. Theoretically, according to local unwritten law, a person of any color could drink in that particular bar; it was our one concession to the concept of the well-heralded American melting pot. Very rarely did white people enter, however, and what little mingling occurred between blacks and Latin-Americans may not have been comfortable. The "Meskin," though not discriminated against quite as openly as was the Negro, was himself segregated in matters of housing and (with rare exceptions) schooling. He competed with Negroes for the community's least desirable jobs. The better restaurants did not want him, nor did Protestant churches approve his worshiping of pagan "idols." Some Latins exhibited their own racist attitudes in bitterly resenting being considered by the *gringo* as little or no better than "niggers." As too often happens, the two oppressed minority groups fought among themselves rather than against their common oppressors.

The Mexican proprietor was made appropriately uncomfortable by the appearance of two tipsy white boys, though he consented to serve us when I flashed papers showing my military commitment and then explained that his place had the honor to host my farewell party. There were only three blacks present (a soldier escorting two young women) along with perhaps a half-dozen old Mexican men conversing in their musical language over bottles of Carta Blanca; two or three young Mexican couples bunched around a rear table. I encountered the black soldier near a juke box specializing in Latin airs. Proudly I remarked that on the morrow I too would be in uniform. "Oh yeah?" he said, which apparently exhausted his interest. He turned back to his table.

I was angry at being so rudely cut, and on returning to our booth advised Burton of a bruised ego. Burton had a reputation for a hair-trigger temper and quick fists. His immediate suggestion was "We should stack this fucking place." Our rising voices caused a general stir; the alarmed host rushed over. "We are all friends here," he proclaimed. "If we have trouble the police come, and all troublemakers go to jail." He cooled us with complimentary beers, though Burton continued to favor the soldier's table with hard stares and mutterings. Eventually, on the grounds of Burton's obviously youthful appearance and because he had no papers linking him to the military, the proprietor enlisted my support in persuading him to leave before lawmen might happen by for an inspection. "They find that white kid drunk in here," the worried beer merchant said, "and they gonna lock up everybody."

I remained, after a sentimental boozy good-by to my old chum, he who had dissected frogs with me in biology, he who had giggled with me in the back row of sophomore English at the foolish affectations of poets, he who had expertly kicked in the groin the Odessa linebacker he caught in careless application of an elbow against my blocking nose. At closing time I could hardly negotiate my freedom from the booth and, once free, tended to wobble more than to walk. The agitated barkeep steered me outside, jumping back in time to avoid the rush of foul liquids boiling up from my nervous belly and sourly splashing on the parched West Texas earth. He supported me while I bent over, a victim of painful dry heaves. Out of some mist, fog, pain, and yellowish light the black soldier and his lady companions appeared. I was first made aware of their presence when the barkeep, pleading that we were both the property of Uncle Sam, urged the soldier to assume my custody.

"*Hell* no!" the experienced old soldier voted. "He need the practice—nobody gonna be around to Mama his ass after tonight. First Sergeant catch him like that, he gonna give him something to puke *about*."

"Piss on you," I said from the dizzy outer rim of death.

"No trouble, no trouble," the poor barkeep coached. "You go," he instructed the soldier. Then he showed a novelist's imagination: "This boy, his father is important in town. A big man like that, he can make trouble for everybody. Come on, you go."

The soldier and his companions departed.

I was pointed in the direction of white precincts and nudged toward home, scuffling along unsteadily, the frequent target of barking dogs. Perhaps an hour later, perhaps two or three, I awoke on a strange lawn several blocks off my homeward course, shaking alternately with chills and fevers. I eventually made it to the night watchman's home and tumbled quickly into bed on a rear sleeping porch, discouraging my worried mother through mumbled assurances of *No, I'm fine, Mom, I'm all right, don't turn on the light, go back to bed, I'll see you in the morning.* Then I lapsed into a feverish, restless sleep. So passed my last night as a citizen in my father's house.

# ii
# The Young
# Warrior

"Caleb," I asked, "are white people people?"

"What are you talking about, Leo?"

"I mean—are white people—*people?* People like us?"

He looked down at me. His face was very strange and sad. It was a face I had never seen before. We climbed a few more stairs, very slowly. Then, "All I can tell you, Leo, is—well, *they* don't think they are."

—James Baldwin, *Tell Me How Long the Train's Been Gone*

**A**week later I was numb from my new understanding of a fact uncovered in turn by all the soldiers of history: the world is not best judged by its recruiting posters. Hardly had my innocent civilian feet touched the earth at Goodfellow Field, our reception center, when a sergeant shouted in harsh and unfamiliar accents, "Aw right, Plowboy, youse wouldn't know a military secret if youse seen one wearing a red necktie. Knock off the friggin' rubber-neckin' and fall inta the friggin' ranks." Two dozen of us, white to a man, were marched raggedly off in the stifling August heat to examinations meant to determine whether our knees would properly jerk when smashed by a rubber hammer and whether we were capable of coughing without pain while medics squeezed our young testicles. After tests to ascertain whether we could read or write passably (two of our number became casualties here, as against one who failed when he betrayed a hernia by crying out during the nut-squeezing ceremonies), we were herded into musty old wooden barracks for our first lessons in GI bed-making, floor swabbing, and urinal polishing.

We had fed from puberty on war movies, where improbable heroes routinely accomplished their impossible glories; we were all volunteers, unlettered young refugees from the oil patch or hard-scrabble ranches or high schools where we had established no new scholastic standards, and we were eager to carry on in the tradition of Sergeant York or Audie Murphy. We knew in our hearts that our Jap-killing rights had been prematurely surrendered by General Douglas MacArthur on the decks of the U.S.S. *Missouri* almost exactly a year earlier, and we perhaps felt both saddened and cheated.

We were generously, exceptionally, uniformly ignorant. Though we had been hazed and cussed by experts in their roles as oil-field tool dressers or ambitious football coaches, we were surprised at our maltreatment in the bosom of our Uncle Sam. When Abbott and Costello had been hazed in *Buck Privates,* we considered it improbable comedy that never could happen to real red-blooded American boys. Certainly we had no idea that Sergeant York or Audie Murphy may have been subjected in their respective times to the sarcasms or whims of common corporals; we did not perceive that mass responsive conditioning and mass dehumanization are necessary processes if awkward young men are to become efficient robots who willingly kill or offer themselves as candidates for death on the word of unseen congressmen, generals, or diplomats. We had no suspicion that psychology existed in the world, and if we had learned of its existence we surely would have wondered at its purpose. We felt, however, those inadequacies and guilts our superiors intended us to experience: had recruits in all recorded history ever had so many left feet, so few brains, such a shortage of the good materials of heroes? Where had we been when Uncle Sam really *needed* us? Why, giggling in study hall or safe at the Battle of Popcorn Bay while up there on the silver screen Errol Flynn marched and bled and died for us not once but many times over.

In the evenings we were permitted until midnight the wild freedoms of San Angelo's more rickety cafés and beer joints, where we frantically tried to convince ourselves that we were not the mindless shitbirds they named us by day. We drank far more than our experiences permitted, poured coins into the juke box to encourage Hank Williams or Ernest Tubb to drown out the echo of our most recent humiliations, fed complimentary drinks and corny lines to aging doxies who knew how to avoid our friendly assaults as they had known how to handle our fathers before us. Our frustrations were thus fed by dark as effectively as by day. Hordes of Military Policemen, wise to the ways and anxieties of raw recruits, swarmed in to check our passes, intervene in the fist fights that exploded like sudden summer storms, and drive us like dazed cattle to the midnight buses of olive drab.

There was an Old Soldier among us, a former combat infantryman advertised as owning a Purple Heart and a Bronze Star, who after a few disappointing months "on the outside" was coming back to the Army as gratefully as a weary traveler might reach home. He felt compelled to make clear his superiority over us despised young "rooks," which he accomplished by sneers, curses, threats, and by the example of cold-cocking with savage left hooks two barroom civilians whose looks he did not approve. The Old Soldier would be the first of many World War II veterans to relate how cowardly Negroes were in combat, how they claimed to be "night fighters" especially painted for their work (or became "American Indians") in order to ingratiate themselves with European women, how they spread venereal diseases the moment their ships docked, how they deserted in droves and generally were not worth the shot it took to kill them. Much, much later I heard the black soldier's complaints about his World War II treatment: though casualty figures and successes in battle belied the charges of his cowardice or combat inefficiency, most white commands assigned black troops to pick-and-shovel duties, to loading or unloading cargo, or to other mule work; white soldiers aggressively taught civilians in foreign lands that their black comrades were unreliable, dirty or diseased, and of inferior mentalities. One would later learn the desperate lengths to which military authorities would go to prohibit marriages between black soldiers and willing white war brides. And one would learn that one's government and one's newspapers had been reluctant to report or had failed to report more than one messy military race riot during that war so highly advertised as the final crusade to bring justice forever to this world.

Within a week we were processed at the reception center and ticketed on the Trailways Line for Fort Sam Houston, near San Antonio, where other geniuses in khaki would further test our capabilities before marking us for our eventual ports of training. I think that night bus ride to Fort Sam through a series of withered and dry little Texas cow towns, with only crying infants and foul odors intruding on my loneliness, will ever deserve a place among the low moments of history. We arrived after midnight to cadenzas of well-perfected abuse; after we were issued ill-fitting war garments, our superiors shoved a half-dozen of us on the train for shipment to our basic-training tortures in New Jersey. We were all Texans, all white, none as old as nineteen. Long before we reached Ohio, conductors had passed word to bartenders that club-car products, combined with the dizzying motions of the train, tended to make one or more of us vomit. We arrived at Trenton station wrung out, pale, wrinkled, and shorn of all earlier confidence.

Awaiting transportation to Fort Dix, we went into a lunch room. Two black men entered. One sat on a stool to my immediate right. Manning of San Angelo and Edwards of Sweetwater lifted their eyebrows, watching carefully to see what I would do.

Fifteen years later, visiting home, I was piously lecturing my relatives on the insanities of racial exclusions when my mother laughed and said, "Lawrence, do you remember when some niggers set down by you the first day you got up to New Jersey? And what a fuss you made?"

"Whatever do you mean?" I asked.

Mother returned from rummaging in an old trunk, bringing a letter I barely recognized to be in my own hand:

*Dear Folks. Got here Thursday on the train from Ft. Sam. We no more than set down in the depot to eat than some niggers plopped down next to us and I can tell you they didn't stay long. We told them we were from Texas and we didn't go for that stuff, and believe-you-me they cleared out in a hurry. . . .*

It is interesting to speculate on why this fiction was composed, for we had actually eaten our hamburgers in a choked and humble silence.

President Truman had not yet issued his order desegregating the military. Black troops at Fort Dix were fed and quartered apart from us, served by their own PXs and service clubs. Except when we encountered them as they marched out to a rifle range while we marched in from the field, we had no contact. I did not think this peculiar: who recalls seeing John Wayne or Humphrey Bogart assisted in their heroics by black troops as they tamed the Japs or routed Nazis? Had I not known that during World War II black troops rebelled against segregationist practices at Midland Army Air Field by refusing to come out of their barracks one morning (for which they were sprayed by pressurized fire hoses) I would not have suspected that Negro GIs even marginally helped defeat Hitler.

Doing its usual fine job of selecting hairdressers to be mechanics and former teamsters to serve as chefs, the Army dispatched me to Fort Monmouth to flunk out of cryptography school, radio operator's school, and radio repair school. Fort Monmouth did, however, introduce me to racial integration, though only our "service" troops (cooks, bakers, supply-room toilers) were black. Here too I came face to face with my first black officer and felt a moment of panic while old prejudices struggled with newly acquired military disciplines: then I snapped him a proper salute.

The only black man among the service troops I came to know more than slightly was Brewster, a cook from Alabama. Where most of us had less than a year's military service, Brewster had ten; he had served in France, and had several times reached the rank of sergeant only to be restored to lower stations after certain picky military regulations had been strictly interpreted. "I been busted for drinkin' and I been busted for thinkin'," he liked to say, "and thinkin' get you in boo-coo more trouble."

"Yawl goddamn privates shut your faces and let us private first classes get our rest," he might sing out from cooks' quarters shortly after lights-out. The white troops would laugh and say ole Brewster was something else, a real card, a good goddamn nigger.

On weekends I became a regular visitor, sitting on Brewster's footlocker while we drank vodka from paper cups, chasing it with tins of GI fruit juices he had liberated from the mess hall. Brewster was full of outrageous tales of the women he had loved from Mobile to Pigalle, the officers he had outwitted, the big deals he had temporarily enjoyed before they mysteriously turned to clabber. He also confessed, in the same high glee, to his own victimizations and defeats. I now know he had a marvelous sense of the absurd and cunning instincts for survival. Even in the 1940s I realized that Brewster was brighter than most people I had known, more complex, full of more hidden secrets and silent victories. Though this worried me as being against the Lord's intent, I continued to sit at his feet.

One night the vodka passed back and forth enough to help some old inhibitions fly away; I found myself drinking from the same bottle with the black man, not bothering to wipe the neck off, and feeling a little noble and extremely daring. I blurted out a question: "What's it really like to be a . . . a Knee-Grow in a white outfit?"

Brewster paused with the vodka bottle near his mouth and stared into my eyes. "It's all right," he said, slowly. "If you ain't got no pride." After a few throbbing seconds of silence he burst into laughter. I was vastly relieved, because then I could laugh too. At exactly what I did not know.

The Army suspended its segregated customs in stockades where prisoners served time for breaches of military etiquette —perhaps to demonstrate to what low estate troublemakers might sink. One day I drew detail as a prisoner chaser. My duty was to trail three stockade baddies with an M-1 rifle while they emptied garbage cans and ashcans into a truck for disposal in the post incinerators. Rumor had it that if one permitted a prisoner to escape, he must serve the balance of the escapee's time. I drew three long-termers: a tall, round-shouldered black man and two white men. I somehow assumed that the black man was the potential jailbreaker; through the morning I kept my M-1 so nervously at the ready that had he sneezed unannounced it might have cost him his liver.

We had started our third or fourth trip to the incinerators when our driver suddenly applied the brakes to avoid running a stop sign. I catapulted across the truck bed, bouncing off my charges, my rifle sailing away. One horrible thought occurred: *I'll be killed now or court-martialed later.* Frantically I struggled up, shedding ashes, egg shells, and old orange peels, to find myself staring into the barrel of my deadly M-1—and the tall black man behind it. "Bang!" my prisoner said, softly, before handing my weapon back. "Hey, driver," he called out, laughing fit to break a stitch. "Be careful up there—you goddamn near killed my guard, and it would of went on my record."

In the spring of 1947, when Jackie Robinson was a new star with the Brooklyn Dodgers and the first black baseball player in the major leagues, I was threatened with shipment to the Army of Occupation in Germany, where, a stern major promised, I might anticipate frequent KP, the "honor" of guard duty as a routine, and the permanent rank of private. Pentagon gods were slightly kinder: I was ordered to the Signal Corps Photo Center in Astoria, Long Island, and soon discovered the sophistications of Times Square, a Brooklyn telephone operator, and any number of friendly taverns throughout the several boroughs.

The arrival of black troops at the Photo Center coincided with my own. They were to be methodically assimilated: to sit with us at table, sleep alongside us, and be assigned jobs without regard to color. Lieutenant Ken Thomas, a slim and erect young North Carolinian, was company commander; I was, in effect, his administrative aide from the moment it was discovered that I had the ability to operate a typewriter without bruising both thumbs. "Washington orders this thing to work," Lieutenant Thomas said of our integrated unit. "They've assigned me a Negro first sergeant. The white troops may resent him. I won't tolerate any unmilitary displays. I hear any racial slurs around here, I'll be mighty hard to live with."

First Sergeant Percy, a native of rural Georgia, had more than a decade in the Army. Though he carried himself with careful dignity, I would soon learn his private fears. "When a man is colored he can't do everything he like to do," Sergeant Percy confided. "I never served with white troops before. They've never served with my kind. Everybody got to step real easy. We can't let the troops know we're walking on eggshells, though. I wear a Top's stripes and draw a Top's pay, and I'm gonna act like a Top."

Perhaps not fully appreciating the problem, I said, "You've got the rank. Use it."

Sergeant Percy's smile was a bit cynical. "Someday," he said, "some white GI gonna bow his ass up at what I got to tell him. Then I'll need a little white rank in here to back me up. I'm recommending Lieutenant Thomas make you corporal immediately, and sergeant sixty days later—if you work out. You don't work out, you can go soldier for somebody that need you."

My relationship with Sergeant Percy was proper and generally easy—though not until years later would I realize we had not been the close friends I once presumed. We listened to baseball on the radio (bantering over whether to tune in "his" newly integrated Dodgers or "my" then segregated Giants) and occasionally each went to see his favorite—but we never went to a game together. Though we shared a table in the mess hall and talked over drinks in my private squad room after retreat formation, he never invited me to his off-base apartment, nor do I recall asking him to an evening on the town. I gave him a wedding gift, but was not invited (nor did I consider that I might be) to the ceremony. Shortly after Sergeant Percy announced his nuptials, I heard two senior sergeants discussing the big social event in the company day room. "I'm kinda surprised ole Percy's gettin' married by a parson," said one, a Southerner. "Down home, niggers that think they're in love generally just jump over a broomstick." "Maybe he had to marry it to git it," his companion suggested. "Well," said the first soldier, "I might marry that gal myself if God had made me black. I seen her once, and she was all legs and pure poontang."

A frequent embarrassment was old Sergeant Smitty, a thirty-year man, serving his final hitch before retirement, whom we loosely utilized as company runner. By noon, Sergeant Smitty had paid several duty calls on the nearby Studio Bar, where he was known for his partiality to rotgut bourbon chased by draft beer. By midafternoon his old face was fire-red, his shirt flapped out over his bloated belly, and he literally drooled tobacco juices, while spinning as many yarns about the glories of the Old Army as his slurred speech permitted.

Sergeant Smitty invariably committed the same racial indiscretion. Halfway through some tale of his triumphs as a youthful mule-skinner in Panama, or while relating a particularly satisfying old debauchery in the Orient's sin palaces, he would refer to one or another "nigger." Then general tensions would cause him to suspect he had done something wrong or out of joint. His besotted old brain would grapple with the mystery as he wheezed and tottered in confusion, blinking at Sergeant Percy until he could recognize him as black. "I'm sorry, Sarjint," he invariably said—and never without a certain shy shame—"I plumb forgot you're Colored." Sergeant Percy routinely responded, "That's all right, Sergeant. Sometimes I forget it myself."

Young Lieutenant Porterfield was Officer of the Day when two drunken GIs engaged in a bloody fistfight. One was white and the other black, but no racial slurs were delivered. Neither did the racially mixed spectators jump into the fight—which had originated over who owned how much liquor remaining in a common jug. Lieutenant Porterfield, however, became flustered; he spoke to the Charge of Quarters loudly enough for all to hear. "We're sitting on a powder keg. All we need to kick off a bloody race riot is one incident like this. I tell you, it won't work."

Sergeant Percy was icily furious in protesting to Lieutenant Thomas. "Sergeant Smitty's just old and ignorant and don't know no better. But that Lieutenant Porterfield, he *supposed* to be an officer and a gentleman." Privately he railed, "Race riot, shit! The only way we gonna have a race riot is if peckerwoods like that Porterfield talk us into one."

The day came when I received my own comeuppance. A cute black chick employed at the Photo Center began to find excuses to visit the Orderly Room, determinedly flirting with Sergeant Percy. One day he grumbled that he wished the lady would cease her attentions because he wasn't "available."

"*I* am," I said. "Why don't you fix me up?"

"Sure I will," he said, coolly. "Then maybe you'll take me to Texas on furlough and fix me up with one of your friends." For the next few days we were excessively cordial.

In August, on a weekend outing to Jones Beach, aided by my share of the communal beer, I slept for hours under the sun and was admitted to the post hospital with severe burns. Then followed painful recuperations in my squad room. Twice each day, by holding to supporting objects, I managed to anoint the seared flesh with prescribed lotions and salves. Since a trip to the mess hall was as impossible as sliding down a fire pole, Sergeant Percy saw that KPs brought trays to my quarters.

One day a young black man from Philadelphia looked in. Twice a day for about two weeks Private First Class Robinson called to sweep and mop my room, change the linens, carry out laundry; sometimes he brought snacks or magazines. We talked about sports, Robinson's foul luck in not having been selected for Officer Candidate School, and my own wish to quit the military.

I was suspicious of Robinson's attentions. Why would a black man devote so much labor to a white man he hardly knew, especially a white man suffering because his inferior skin pigments offered no natural defenses against the sun? Perhaps he wanted favors I might bestow as company clerk: KP with less frequency than normal, an occasional three-day pass, a cushy job. I even considered the possibility that Robinson's attentions might be sexual. As time passed and he asked no favors of my office or of my flesh, my suspicions changed to curiosity. One night I stammered thanks. "Don't mention it," he said. "This is part of my life's work." I thought this over while Robinson expertly pushed the mop back and forth: "What were you in civilian life? A porter?" Robinson gave me a strange, unbelieving look. "No, Sergeant," he said. "I was a student in a seminary, studying to become a minister. I've had three years of college." He never came back.

Several times I hinted to black soldiers with whom a certain rapport was assumed of my willingness to accompany them on one of their journeys to Harlem. These generous offers were met with vague references to some unspecified future.

Harlem was a foreign port in the mind, an exotic paradise where Clark Gable, conveniently shipwrecked, cavorted with dusky dancing belles while some fat, jolly chieftain urged on him feasts of suckling pig and ritual tribal honors. One adventurous evening I determined to explore New York's dark interior in the absence of a native guide. Three other white crackers (from Georgia, West Virginia, and Texas) accompanied me. We ordered a reluctant white cabbie to deliver us to "the heart of Harlem." "It's no skin offa my ass," the cabbie said, "but I won't be surprised when the Army comes up four soldiers short tomorrow. Them damn niggers gonna rob you blind and leave you dead in a alley." Harlem had not always been such deadly ground: in the good old days white people had been encouraged to enjoy the hospitality of the better bistros such as the old Cotton Club, where the jazz greats played, or had been welcome on special evenings at the Apollo Theater. But now (our cabbie said) all that had changed: ignorant and uppity niggers had come boiling up from the South dragging their cottonfield resentments behind them, niggers with smart mouths, niggers who stayed North no more than thirty days before getting it in their heads they were as good as white people.

Harlem was not the kind of street carnival I had imagined. There were the old eyesores and dangers one would later come to expect in other black ghettos: sorry old tenement buildings, peeling and rotting in dull reds and grays; pawnshops with their pitiful treasures locked behind iron grills; hole-in-the-wall liquor stores with gaudy displays of half pints; storefront missions smelling of sweat and disinfectants; poor restaurants specializing in chicken wings or cheap barbecue plates; crowded, noisy bars wailing soul music above the human babble; clots of gutter trash and street debris.

We had not advanced a block before a comely young hooker accosted us. While we stood making uneasy conversation a sharply dressed Negro man approached and scolded the streetwalker: "You got more sense than to hustle them here. You trying to get somebody hurt? Go on over to Chunky's to hustle your ass." And to us: "Get on out from here. This a bad-ass street and it won't do nothing for you."

We fled rapidly down the sidewalk, fending off happy drunks who invited us to buy them drinks and sullen ones demanding money. A grossly fat woman in a silk print dress dashed from a door to damn us in a raging, profane gibberish. Cool-eyed dudes in padded-shouldered sports coats, tapered trousers, and porkpie hats offered to provide certain recreations at only slight profits to themselves—and one just knew, just *understood,* that to follow them into a dark doorway would fulfill our cabbie's prophecy. Street urchins howled and danced with their hands out, berating us when our conciliatory contributions proved miserly beyond their expectations. A drunk in tattered clothing sipped the last dregs from a wine bottle. He offered his hand, and as one of our number reached to take it the drunk laughed and broke the wine bottle under our feet, showering us with glass particles and wine droplets.

We ducked into a bar where a dozen men and women laughed and talked above the throbbing juke box. All sounds except the music seemed to stop as we entered, doubtless look-

ing a bit panicky and trying to cover up by affecting a bluster-
ing chatter. "The Marines have landed," somebody hooted. My
companion from West Virginia didn't help by responding, "Marines, my ass, Mac! We're soldiers."

The bartender hesitated when we ordered beers, but he finally produced them. He kept a close watch, however, and came
quickly when a slight, reed-thin man the color of lightly
creamed coffee, imagining we were staring too openly at his
lady friend, cursed us as "goddamn mother-fuckin' white
hunters"—i.e., white men on the prowl for black women.

Aided by the aroused citizen's lady, the bartender persuaded
him to move to a distant table where he might find us less offensive. Then the bartender leaned across the bar: a burly, middle-aged, slick-bald man. "What you boys lost in Harlem?" he
demanded. Not waiting for an answer he said, "Some places in
Harlem you can go and everything be just dandy. This ain't one
of 'em. All you gonna find here is trouble—hot weather like
this, shit, it just *breed* meanness. People get all hot and sticky
and about half out of their heads."

He snapped and crackled a bar rag, scowling. "You boys got
money for a taxi?" We nodded. "I'll phone you a taxi and you
ride on out of here."

Safely back in midtown Manhattan, we speculated on the
reasons for our hostile reception. West Virginia saw no riddle:
niggers were niggers and could be expected to act like niggers.
Georgia, who had done a hitch in Army Counterintelligence,
was mindful of the Communist influences pervading Harlem.
My Texas friend, of a genteel and moneyed old family, felt that
much of what we had seen and heard could be attributed to a
lack of proper breeding. I thought that possibly all three of my
companions were a little bit correct.

Staff Sergeant Hutchinson, a black man from Louisiana, had
several years exemplary service when family problems turned
him into an habitual AWOL. He explained why he needed

emergency leave: "My wife, she pretty young and I been away in the Army so much and now trouble has come. I think a leave straighten her out. We can talk, it might get her thinkin' on our babies again."

Lieutenant Thomas granted the emergency leave and several subsequent ones. Sergeant Hutchinson's allotted leave time expired; his domestic torment did not. Higher brass refused additional leaves, so Hutchinson skipped over the hill. He was let off with company punishment. For subsequent offenses, however, he was reduced to private and sent to the military stockade on Governors Island, where he spent his rare spare hours writing ineffective letters begging a hardship discharge. Within a week after completing each sentence, Hutchinson would disappear. FBI agents, with no more Nazi spies to shadow, and not yet fully clued by J. Edgar Hoover and Senator Joe McCarthy to the internal Communist menace, were in those days efficient tracers of runaway soldiers; probably a detective with no more credentials than a ten-cent Junior G-Man Badge could have swiftly located Hutchinson, for he invariably headed straight for his shanty on the edge of a rotting little Louisiana town. If the Feds didn't arrive at his doorstep before he did, Hutchinson could be trailed to a slaughterhouse where he specialized in scalding and plucking newly murdered chickens. The third or fourth time he was apprehended, I was sent to a stockade near Shreveport to return him under guard.

Master Sergeant Bad ran his stockade much as I imagine Hitler commanded the Third Reich. He was broad, florid-faced, a ham-handed son of Ohio, and a former deputy sheriff; one here had to revise upward one's estimations of the Army's talent for typecasting. He received me while relaxing among his private collection of handcuffs, zip guns, switchblade knives, and rubber truncheons artistically mounted on beaverboard behind his desk. He was drinking coffee served by an obsequious prisoner who bowed out of the room as if departing the odor of royalty. "Prisoners are shit!" Master Sergeant Bad thundered at the bowing lackey. "Sound off!" "Prisoners are shit!" the lackey obediently bawled.

Reading my orders M/Sgt. Bad said, "That's a smart-ass nigger you've come after, Sarjint." Well, I said, Hutchinson had been a good soldier before his family torments. "He tried that sob-sister shit on me," Bad said. "I told him if his old lady was humpin' outside the home he wasn't no worse off than half the white men I know and all the niggers."

He entertained me with stories of all the heads he had been privileged to knock in the service of his country. Criminal types could never be rehabilitated beyond their lower instincts: "They just like a bad buckin' bronco or a mean dawg. You got to clobber the puredee shit out of 'em often enough they'll remember who's boss." Niggers, he advised, were more troublesome than whites: they didn't feel as much pain, and they had shorter memories.

M/Sgt. Bad led me through three locks and past a cadre of guards. As we approached the bullpen where Hutchinson and other transient offenders bunked, he bellowed, "Prisoners, *up!*" There was a wild stampede of nervous sweaty flesh; the prisoners sprinted into a single long rank facing the door and perhaps six feet from the bars. "You're drag-assin', you're drag-assin'," the sergeant accused. "Come again! Fall out!" The prisoners rushed back to their assigned bunks, straining and grunting. Some had not yet reached their proper places when their master thundered, "Prisoners, *up!*"—again inspiring the frantic scramble. Bad ran the prisoners through the exhausting exercise again and again, explaining in convenient asides his and the Pentagon's theory that the more miserable life is for a prisoner the less likely he is to repeat old offenses.

When the prisoners had lined up to his satisfaction M/Sgt. Bad spat, "Prisoner Six . . . *toe the line!*" Hutchinson leaped from the ranks as if kicked, his toes exactly touching a thin red line extending the length of the cell and ending no more than a foot from the bars. "They fuck up and step on that line or anticipate my command," Bad said, "and I treat 'em to a little practice with some ass-paddlin' on the side. We call it a piss party." He raised his voice, "Prisoners, do I give good piss parties? Sound off!"

"Yessir!" the prisoners shouted, with such enthusiasm one might have thought him a rival of Perle Mesta.

"Had one old jug-butted boy never *did* learn to toe the line without steppin' on it," the Sergeant said. "Dumb goddamn nigger! He come here weighing two hunnert pounds and left with a skinny ass didn't have nothing on it but calluses and blood." He chuckled, much cheered by the memory.

Hutchinson had unfortunately relaxed his West Point brace; just as he cut his eyes ever so slightly toward us, M/Sgt. Bad screamed, "What you wallin' them maroon eyes at, you burr-headed bastard? Goddamn your black hide, you're in my custody till I sign your release slip. I tell you to eat shit you *eat* it, right? Sound off!"

"Yessir!" Hutchinson barked.

"You're a smartass runaway nigger, ain't you? Sound off!"

"Yessir!"

"You got shit for brains and piss in your blood. Sound off!"

"Yessir!"

Hutchinson was forced to affirm every insult M/Sgt. Bad was capable of delivering. Nothing was out of bounds: Hutchinson's race, sex habits, wife, and mother. Marching the prisoner to the office, his tormentor prodded him in the ribs with a nightstick—presumably the better to improve his inferior memory. While he signed papers to transfer the prisoner to my control, he warned Hutchinson what might happen to his black ass should it ever again know that particular stockade.

Hutchinson remained discreetly silent while a driver delivered us to the Shreveport train station. When we were alone he said, "Man, I'm gladder to see you than Christmas. That Sergeant Bad, he the meanest mutha in uniform. Especially if you Colored." Had he actually hit Hutchinson? "Name me a day he didn't," the black man said. (Later, when I delivered Hutchinson to Governors Island to await his next court-martial, and he was being stripped for processing, a ferret-faced white corporal grinned at welts and bumps on his back and shoulders. "I guess you got those falling in the shower, didn't you?" "Yessir!" Hutchinson said.)

Down in Louisiana, handcuffed to my prisoner as regulations prescribed, I had boarded the train; we took seats near the rear of a coach car. A conductor approached, apprehensively eying my sidearm. "You gonna have to take him to the Colored section," he said, pointing at Hutchinson. No, my prisoner would go where I went—and I was not going to any Colored section.

There was a delay while the Shreveport station sent reinforcements. A civilian with a public-relations smile and a squishy handshake was full of soft Southern assurances that he knew I would understand and sympathize with the railroad's position in honoring local customs. No, I did not, and would remain in place with my prisoner. The baffled railroaders, faced with conflicting authority, decided in favor of the man with the gun: "But really, suh, the dining car *must* be off limits. Any violation will unfortunately require the police."

Hutchinson slept or feigned sleep, arousing only to share the gummy sandwiches and tepid soft drinks purchased from an aisle barker, or to visit the washroom with his guard closely trailing. After each trip a black porter, called by the alert conductor, entered the washroom for purposes of fumigation. "Hello, Brother," he said in a whisper to Hutchinson on each occasion.

A skinny white man in a short-sleeved sport shirt, with the seedy look of a failed road drummer, a real-life Willy Loman working the Southern Territory, grew talkative as he siphoned off bourbon in the seat behind us. He leaned forward to cool our faces with whiskey breezes while telling how the white man had busted a gut to help the Nigra but the Nigra wouldn't help himself: refused work, stayed drunk or in jail, stole with more talent than Gypsies. "Don't you know that boy's closer to Heaven right now than most niggers ever get? Riding with white folks, havin' 'em look after him." When I replied that Hutchinson's care was provided at gunpoint, and therefore might not be fully appreciated, he looked on me with suspicion. Soon he began whispering around the car: why was that damned black nigger outlaw allowed to ride in the same coach with patriotic, God-fearing white people? A conductor moved the troublemaker to another car when I explained that should he further disturb me or my prisoner it would be both my sworn duty and my personal pleasure to shoot him.

At Washington the train became racially integrated. Hutchinson was vastly relieved: "Man, I'm glad to be rid of them peckerwoods. All that shit about me being in Heaven. . . ."

I apologized for the peckerwood's remarks, noting that I had silenced him and had him moved. You're back among friends, I said, so relax.

"You didn't do me no favors bringing me up on that white car, Sarjint," Hutchinson said. "I would rather have rode with my own people."

Such a possibility had not occurred to me.

I did not walk around New York counting Negroes, and so must now rely on general impressions almost twenty-five years old. I recall seeing few black people on the streets in Queens and fewer still in jobs. My favorite bars showed predominately Irish, Italian, or German influences; rare was the black customer. I saw no blacks at all on Jones Beach, at Far Rockaway, or in Bayside or Flushing Meadow. Queens was not my favored recreational stomping grounds, however; even a small-town Texan soon learns that Manhattan is advantaged over its sister boroughs.

In those Manhattan saloons a sergeant could marginally afford, blacks were only infrequently encountered. Most of these were private people, drinking alone or in twos or threes, and almost exclusively male. They appeared to be quiet men, careful men, men who perhaps smiled a bit quickly if approached by a strange white man or who took pains to extract themselves from barroom conversations in a manner leaving all the social proprieties intact. They often carried briefcases and wore carefully kept suits; if questioned, they might confess to working for a certain Wall Street brokerage house or midtown department store. Only in later years, reading black writers on their experiences in our white world, would I learn that most such men in the 1940s were almost surely office "boys," messengers, guards, or "custodial engineers"—and that their briefcases likely contained nothing more exotic than their brass-buttoned uniforms or workmen's clothes. Such was their desperate search for status, dignity, respectability.

The closer one came to the dingy little bars on side streets off Times Square, around the bend from shooting galleries, hot-dog stands, or all-night movie houses specializing in skin flicks and resident deviates, the more blacks one found. These were less prosperous in appearance than their brothers in the quieter middle-class hotel bars or cocktail lounges for which I had developed a weakness. They were more dedicated to drink, there was more of the hustler in them, their eyes were red and weary or angry, they were more likely (one sensed) to cut a white boy's gizzard should he offend them in a whiskey moment. There were more black women in these seedier spots, too, not a few of which routinely patrolled the West 40s and 50s offering love for sale. Though I think more white ladies than black were then in the streetwalking profession on that turf, intelligence sources inform me this is no longer true.

Compared to the society in which I had grown up, however, I witnessed a higher percentage of blacks than before in their recreations, in jobs, in ties and suit coats. Not once did I observe a black person being turned out of a bar or restaurant in Manhattan (though I did once in Queens and twice in Brooklyn). No white man called a black one a nigger or a boog or a jig to his face—not in my presence, anyhow. Nor did I see the black man made sport of in that sly way some Southerners enjoy with blacks called as witnesses in court or otherwise suddenly thrust into unfamiliar roles in white institutions. So while I heard more than one cab driver or counterman or bartender or soldier refer to blacks in derogatory terms or deride their abilities or life styles, it really didn't occur to me that New York was a place of excessive prejudices. Had anyone asked in the late 1940s whether New Yorkers discriminated against blacks, I would have been foolish enough to say "No" or "Not very much."

Only when I began to revisit New York in the early 1960s after a fourteen-year absence would I revise my thinking. Then (as now) only token blacks were to be found at the executive level in financial institutions, publishing houses, or other commercial concerns. The black man or woman was more likely a messenger or a switchboard operator than a clerk or secretary, more likely a clerk or secretary than an office supervisor or editorial assistant, more likely an office supervisor or editorial assistant than a junior executive or editor—and their chances increasingly diminished as the scale ascended.

Cab drivers, casual bar-stool acquaintances, even an editor and writer or two seemed in the 1960s more obsessed with volunteering their dislike or suspicion of the black man than formerly. I was capable of experiencing shock in 1967 when, trailing Mayor John Lindsay while preparing an article for *Harper's,* I heard him taunted as a "nigger lover" by a rowdy group of Canarsie teen-agers, and severely chastised by merchants, clerks, and little old ladies of Brooklyn's Bay Ridge section for his alleged "coddling" of blacks. The good burghers of Bay Ridge endorsed a philosophy distressingly familiar and increasingly voiced: the white man worked, sweated, and paid taxes; the black man sat on his duff, happily accepted the dole, howled for the world to be delivered wrapped in cellophane. "Well, we've three hundred years of neglect to repair," the Mayor would begin, and before he had reached the second stanza Bay Ridge eyes glazed over, Bay Ridge feet shuffled impatiently, Bay Ridge lips formed sneers. I later remarked to Mayor Lindsay that until recent years I had presumed white prejudice to be almost the exclusive property of the South. Lindsay laughed without any mirth: "Hell, there are bigots in New York as well as in Alabama. You should hear the wild shit they shout at me in Queens."

But to return to the New York of mid-1948. My youthful heart was temporarily in ill repair, having been broken by the Brooklyn telephone operator whose Old Country parents (Italian, and Catholic to a fault) convinced her of the earthly trials and eternal fires awaiting should she continue to date a drawling Protestant from Texas in whose family blood some special Southern insanity surely flowed unchecked. I made a real production of this romantic rejection, mooning around for weeks, drinking so much medical alky one night that they came with the stomach pump, after which I took to my bed much in the manner of the spurned heroine of a Victorian novel. The young heal quickly, however, and soon I drifted into the therapeutic company of an aspiring young actress newly arrived in New York from the Missouri side of Kansas City.

Electa shortly introduced me to Greenwich Village, where I knew my first show folk, struggling authors, lesbians, marijuana experiments, and revolutionary dialogue; if such a varied show was meant to dazzle a country boy it surely succeeded. On spellbound evenings in one or another walk-up flat or scabby loft in the Village, I blinked through bluish hazes from cigars, cigarettes, and now and again a pipe or home-rolled object, trying to make some sense of what was being said, trying to key those strange new sermons of life to the contrary preachments of my Texas youth. People casually quoted lengthy passages of what I half-suspected was Shakespeare, or snatches of what I feared might be Marx (for at our weekly troop-orientation lectures back at the Signal Corps Photo Center our authorities were beginning to teach us the handy art of spotting Reds on sight or by sound). Many conversations were so wholly outside my frames of reference or experience that I simply had no mental yardstick by which to measure the moment's philosophy.

I would sit all goggle-eyed and wondering, surreptitiously moving about to avoid my natural turn at the marijuana joint, for I was convinced it reeked of "dope." And everyone knew that dope made folks jump screaming from high places, sell their bodies to white slavers, or carve up their grandmothers with bread knives.

The bohemian crowd to which I became uneasily attached was more democratic than most in its racial attitudes. Our gatherings sometimes produced several blacks aspiring to one or another of the arts—hopeful actors or actresses, unappreciated poets, marginally employed or unemployed musicians. I did not see enough of them, or feel comfortable enough in the presence of their strange ideas, to form any lasting friendships: blacks seemed to have a higher rate of turn-over in the group than did their white bohemian brothers or sisters. Phil failed to publish and returned home to Indianapolis; Alice went off with a quartet of touring singers; Richard married and disappeared into the straight world as one of several assistants to a department-store window dresser after finding no roles on or off Broadway; Janet simply disappeared.

Talk of racial differences or problems was not fashionable. Some wry reference might be made by a black man to his fortunate escape from the South, or some quick offense might flash in a dark eye should I too suddenly introduce my twangy Texas accent in new social circumstances. Generally, however, talk ranged from books I had not read through the Progressive Party hopes of Henry Wallace to Jackie Robinson's feats with the Brooklyn Dodgers; little was injected of racial ferment or injustices. Such reforms as were in the air seemed to deal with general economic matters: something vague about a rising of "the masses," a mysterious uplifting of the unspecified "working classes"—though it's possible many subtleties of semantics escaped the young man I then was. "What do they talk about?" a G.I. friend asked as I tried to explain this puzzling new world into which I had stumbled. "Well," I said, "things." "What kind of things?" "Just . . . *things!*" I was trying to say that these new people talked primarily of ideas, an experience so alien that I could give it no name.

Though interracial couples were not plentiful, I encountered them for the first time. My first such sight neither shook me to the roots nor struck me blind: the arrangement was a white man with a black woman. Eventually, however, a couple reversed the sexual color patterns—and I found myself reacting strangely. Inside my white boy's craw I was resentful, fearful, perhaps a little sickened. Here was living evidence of what I had heard whispered: black men lusted for white flesh above barbecue or watermelon; they were sexually insatiable; their dongs were without exception the tools of brutes. ("I killed me a rattlesnake the other day purty near as long as ole Joe Louis's dick," I had heard an old farmer say in my Uncle Claude's barbershop back in Putnam.) Not for some time would the sight of a black man with his white woman fail to stir some deeply rooted old deposit of poisons in my soul. Not for longer still (and by processes so slow that I can't pinpoint when it happened) would I honestly approve or simply not give a damn about something that was properly none of my business anyway. I had no objection, of course, to convenient liaisons between white men and black women: this was part of the accepted white sub-culture, so long as one didn't bring home a social disease, fall in love, or flaunt one's black lady in the white community's face.

When I left the Army in mid-1949, the Photo Center had suffered no major racial incidents. Private Reese, ultimately cashiered out with a Bad Conduct discharge because of his uncontrollable drinking, inspired a minor flurry one dawn by launching a drunken kicking, hitting, spitting attack upon inanimate objects which he addressed in screaming tones as "You goddamn Jew footlocker" and "You goddamn nigger GI fartsack." Everyone by then knew that Private Reese had successfully pickled his brain and saw parades of tiny pink elephants and large polka-dot snakes, so little account was taken of the matter. I came to consider our integrated "experiment" a success. In retrospect, I recognize it for the timid compromise or careful accommodation that it was.

For all his bold talk of "acting like a Top" and treating everyone uniformly, I now know that Sergeant Percy gave more severe tongue-lashings or punishments to erring black soldiers than to whites. On the other hand, I spoke softly to black soldiers in need of company discipline, while leaning heavily on whites who I feared might give Sergeant Percy difficulty. Our reverse-racist policy was not a matter of understanding: it merely evolved out of caution born of our unspoken fears.

It was never suggested that our Enlisted Men's Club host a dance or other social affair which might mingle drinking with social integration between two races and two sexes. And while, theoretically, we could bring our dates or spouses to the club three nights in the week for drinks or juke-box soundings, few GIs did so. I don't recall ever seeing a black woman there; most white women who were escorted in had generally established their reputations as easily maneuverable in the vicinity of beds.

On base, the troops themselves intermingled freely—or so was the illusion. We played poker and drank together, sometimes exchanging the rough, friendly barracks insults traditional between soldiers. We performed together as equals on the post football, baseball, and basketball teams. (In one game, however, we knew tensions in the huddle after one of our white running backs thoughtlessly urged his linemen to "block that black bastard they got at left end.") On outings when the Army provided transportation to beaches, boxing matches, West Point football games, or other diversions, I recall no particular groupings or divisions by color. When a half dozen white civilian toughs beat and put the boots to two black soldiers in a Queens bar, two dozen of us—black and white—marched on the bar to clean it of Irish influences.

With the benefit of hindsight, however, I recall on many occasions walking up to a group of black soldiers in friendly, ani-

mated conversation—only to see them quickly adopt more formal attitudes, throw up a cautious guard; I had the distinct
impression that there suddenly had been a change in subject
matter. I did not know that since the earliest slave ships landed
in America the black man had of necessity practiced the art of
speaking in two tongues and showing two faces, becoming one
thing in the presence of the white master and another in the
company of his disadvantaged peers.

I did know, without giving it conscious thought, that we
white men presented one face to the black race and another to
our white peers. An old-timer from Arkansas, a balding staff
sergeant, exhibited a friendly countenance to our black comrades. Yet, privately, he complained that a black soldier had
flashed him the secret fraternal Masonic sign: *Why, goddammit,
what did that black bastard mean "buzzing" me that-a-way?
Don't he know that white Masons don't recognize black pre-
tenders to Brotherhood?* A middle-aged civilian who coached
our post boxing team voiced his opinion that most niggers just
didn't come equipped with "fighting hearts": if you could escape damage in the early going with a nigger you almost surely
would whip him because niggers lost their spirit at the first
sight of true adversity. Even knowing that we presented ourselves as one thing when we might be entirely another thing did
not lead me to suspect that *they* might be equally devious. Apparently, I subconsciously considered the white man's superiority to extend even to gifts of social mendacity.

When we left the Photo Center to seek our private
amusements, we rarely saw racially mixed groups troop out the
front gate. I can now recall the names of only a half dozen
blacks with whom I soldiered for more than two years—and
am amazed to realize how little of their personal lives I
learned. We simply didn't know one another.

The night following my military discharge in July 1949, a
captain from upstate New York invited me to the Officers'
Club—forbidden territory so long as I had remained a lowly
Enlisted Man. I had always considered the captain a good man,

giving him credit for his contributions to our integrated post. He seemed genuinely friendly to black troops and had assigned them billets and promotions in his office without apparent bias. For several hours we reveled, other officers joining our table to toast my new civilian status and to wish me luck "on the outside." No black officers were present; despite the careful mix of enlisted troops, only two or three black officers were among the several dozen assigned to the Photo Center—and these were temporary students or held technicians' assignments not even remotely connected with troop command.

Late in the evening my host expressed regrets that I had accepted my discharge: he felt that I was career material. Well, I said, I wanted to attend college and thought perhaps I had it in me to write.

The captain lowered his voice. "I really don't blame you. I might resign my commission if I were younger and didn't have so much time in. There's no future in the Army if they continue to mix the races."

# iii
# Desert Transitions

"Caleb," I asked, "are all white people the same?"

"What do you mean, the same?"

"I mean—you know—are they all the *same?*"

And Caleb said, "I never met a good one."

I asked, "Not even when you were little? In school?"

Caleb said, "Maybe. I don't remember." He smiled at me. "I never met a good one, Leo. But that's not saying *you* won't. Don't look so frightened."

—James Baldwin, *Tell Me How Long the Train's Been Gone*

# P

erhaps the Army's brand of racial integration had its limitations or dirty little secrets, but when I returned to my native Southwest I would again encounter a totally segregated society.

Among the six thousand students then at Texas Tech, in Lubbock, there was not a single black face. Lubbock was one of those growing, sprawling, newly prosperous cities the South and Southwest seemed to spew in the postwar boom—cities rising out of the desert, or from the pine thickets, multiplying themselves for reasons not often apparent. In my old home, Midland, the population had grown from 9,000 in 1940 to 21,000 by 1950, and by 1960 would reach 67,000, causing my father to condemn it for its bright lights, crowded streets, and wicked ways.

I paused briefly in Midland following my Army discharge in 1949, noting the rapid changes of three postwar years on what had been a sleepy little cow town until World War II came along with its need for petroleum exploration and its giant payroll at Midland Army Air Field. New shopping centers sprang up, offering delicacies or services not common to rural Texas tastes: a Brooklyn Italian stationed at Midland Army Field remained to establish the region's first "pizza parlor," an ex-GI from Miami stayed to open the town's first diaper service, and two New York types saw the need for a small advertising agency. Sites I remembered as fields for pickup football or baseball games were now paved over as parking lots or hosting new office buildings; there was a brokerage office where secretaries and draftsmen took their noon hours to play the stock market and study the postings, as their betters did on Wall Street. A new breed had come to town following the war—lawyers or independent oilmen trained in the law classes of Yale or at Harvard Business School. New housing developments were crisscrossed by streets showing the new influence: Harvard Street, Princeton Avenue, Yale Drive. There was oil under the ground and bustle in the air. The young invaders who came to Midland to prosper from the Permian Basin oil strike were adventurers, plungers, men eager to get in on the ground floor and zoom to the top, men unwilling to wait it out in the corporate offices of the East where hundreds walked in hushed shadows while wondering if their names would be seen on the corporate letterhead before turning up on retirement rolls or tombstones. Bob Hope and Greer Garson invested to give Hollywood local representation, as did a combine of football coaches with connections as far-ranging as the University of Texas and the professional Detroit Lions. *Life* magazine did a gee-whiz picture layout on the Midland boom; to pick up the *Reporter-Telegram* in those early postwar years was to be inundated by Boosterism. We achieved a symphony orchestra and a new Little Theater. The gloomy old Scharbauer Hotel lobby—famed for its mounted giant steer horns, cracked leather couches, and brass spitoons, where many a grizzled trail-driver had bargained with local ranchers over the price of their cattle on the hoof—got a face-lifting of fluorescent lights, airy emptiness, and automatic elevators so that (as many a disgruntled old rancher accurately grumbled) you couldn't tell it from one in Cleveland or Miami. I made a brief tour of the Flats and noted that there, at least, nothing had changed: there remained the same dusty or muddy unpaved streets, outdoor privies, creaking lean-tos, and hopeless futures.

One morning I tossed a single suitcase into the back of a friend's pickup truck and motored off to Lubbock, perhaps three hours away, to enroll in Texas Tech. Lubbock, too, had a small and not highly visible black population confined to substandard schools and ghetto living. Though Lubbock then enjoyed advertising itself as "the City of Churches," the boys of Texas Tech could point the way to twenty-odd motels or hotels where prostitutes were for hire, each clearly marked by the black bellhop prominently stationed so as to encourage the cruising trade.

A young, toothy minister full of prattle of his love for Jesus and Jesus' love for all singled me out at a meeting in the Baptist Student Union (to which I had been attracted in the pursuit of a particularly well-stacked young child of God) and asked, "What might we, as Christians, do to better serve the Lord in our daily contacts with others?" I answered something like "End our hypocrisy in treating the black man like a slave or an animal, while claiming fidelity to Christian brotherhood." The young minister's Jesus-loving face caved in, his eyes frosted over; he stuttered aimlessly until someone else suggested that we might visit civic clubs to urge Christian principles on businessmen—which the minister gratefully endorsed.

My lust for the young Baptist flesh bordered on agony. After some weeks of semi-intimate association, during which her virtue remained intact despite numerous moonlight opportunities sent by enemies of the church, I quickly accepted that most ominous of bachelor invitations: to visit her family acres on a convenient weekend for the purpose of meeting Mom and Dad. On our drive up from dusty Lubbock to the wheat and cattle precincts of the flat and lonely Texas Panhandle, to real *Hud* country, I received my social instructions: When Mama asked if I wanted something to drink, now, Mama would be offering nothing more stimulating than Cokes, iced tea, or Kool-Aid. Be sure and mention that we had met at the Baptist Student Union (we had not, but this little white lie would presumably assure nervous parents that I was built of pious clay). Please don't come out with "one of your careless damns or hells." And, oh yes: "Please, *please* don't get to talking like you do about the Nigras. Daddy would faint but Mama might *die!*"

My lady looked fetching in snug blue jeans and a blouse pleasingly endowed. Though I do not recall that my aroused instincts included the matrimonial, when we arrived near sundown at the family ranch it soon became apparent that our common future was assumed in other quarters. While the mother bustled around choosing victims for Cokes or Kool-Aid, a giggly little kid sister blurted, "You gonna marry Carol Jane?" Frantic adult shushings merely reinforced the idea that perhaps this thought was not the sole property of an indiscreet child. A supper of my favorite foods (chicken-fried steak with cream gravy, corn on the cob, coconut cake, home-freezer strawberry ice cream) made it obvious the weekend had been well planned in its small particulars.

The mother's careful post-meal inquisition, touching on my personal ambitions, my family roots, and my degree of commitment to Baptist theology, signaled deeper dangers; instinctively, I grew wary in my responses. When my loins' desire sweetly kissed me good night in front of damaging witnesses before tripping off to a safely remote wing of the ranch house for innocent slumber, I knew a sinking feeling unmatched since discovering that Santa Claus was somebody no more important than Daddy. Nor were my fears allayed when the father led me out on the veranda to volunteer a general accounting of his land holdings, to lament having no sons to succeed him, and endorse Carol Jane's cooking, horsemanship, and church-going qualities. ("Time she was six, she could set a mount like a man. Time she was ten, she had read the New Testament through twice and won a ton of ribbons for memorizing the Scriptures.") Whatever else I then wanted of life, it did not include a pious cowgirl for a bride.

Hours after that terrifying talk on the veranda, I tossed and turned in wonder at how cleverly they had gotten the noose half over my head without my even seeing the rope. What had I said in some moment of moonlight madness out at Palo Duro Canyon, in the flickers of a Baptist Student Union campfire, or struggling and panting in the front seat of my lady's prewar Dodge parked behind Jones Stadium or on some dusty country lane, that could possibly account for this clear and present danger? Like many a young man in such desperate circumstances, I suddenly saw a disturbing physical resemblance between my handsome young lady and her well-girdled mother: Sweet Jesus, was Carol Jane's cute little button nose soon to widen and be surrounded by two powdered mounds of plump asexual flesh, her wide blue eyes to narrow to little pig slits, her shapely legs to grow mysteriously stumpy, her ginger-colored hair that smelled like baby soap to frizzle and go gray? I debated whether to wake the household to hoot and dance in protest of its presumptuous attitudes. But that would be unthinkably embarrassing. I simply had to find more oblique means.

Disgustingly near sunrise, reluctantly and unsteadily mounted on a horse for which I developed no special affinity, I was cantered across the brown family acres in the inspection of prize bulls, wild flowers, fields of wheat stubble, barns, cattle corrals. Shortly before noon my host led me into a hay barn, where he uncovered half a bottle of Old Crow. With a comradely wink he cautioned that our pause for refreshment should not be mentioned in the company of "our womenfolk." "I take a little nip now and again," the old rancher confessed. "I don't hold that whiskey in reasonable amounts hurts a man. 'Course, *too much* of a good thing, now, is gonna ruin anybody."

I grabbed the bottle with both hands, determined to establish myself as a man of excesses. After two or three healthy snorts I offered confessions which hopefully might further establish my high degree of risk: I had never felt as one with the soil; farming and ranching techniques puzzled me as fully as did higher mathematics or the doctrine of Total Immersion; I was sore afraid of the smallest domestic animal; I yearned for bright lights and loud music; possibly small vestiges of Art corrupted my innards because I wanted to be a writer; I even threw in a representative sprinkling of the forbidden damns and hells.

My host disappointed in failing to pronounce me unqualified. Instead, he set about to rehabilitate my thinking. "Well, now," he said, "I don't think Carol Jane much likes the big city. First year down there at Tech, she couldn't hardly sleep for all that traffic whizzing by so close to her dorm. And as for that *writing* business—well, the reporter for our little weekly paper, he works for next to nothing. And he told me one time that even the Amarillo papers don't pay much better."

Encouraged by Old Crow, I revealed that my writing ambitions went beyond anything I had seen published in the Amarillo newspapers: the novel was my destiny, fame was the spur, Hollywood or New York my goal.

*"New York!"* the old rancher exclaimed in tones identifying it with the far edges of hell. "We went up to New York to the World's Fair just before the war, and I couldn't get away from that place quick enough. People all mixed up together, living like rats. And I swear, it looked to me like half of 'em was niggers."

Ah, the magic word. Suddenly, there it was: my sure exit to freedom. Giving the black man one more historic example of the white man misusing him, I said, "Well, I was in the Army with quite a few Negroes. Some of 'em were pretty good men."

"You soldiered with *niggers?*"

Yeah, I had been among the first. And I had liked a number of them, too. Palled around with 'em. Had even been introduced to some few of their sisters. While the old man gorged on the undigestible, I supplied the crusher: "Before I went up to New York, I really didn't know anything about Negroes. I mean, I thought we were *better* than they are. Hell, that's just not true. They're as smart as white people—some of 'em may be a damn sight smarter."

I don't believe the old man would have been more shocked had I pronounced myself gay. Carefully, he capped the jug and returned it to its hiding place behind a hay bundle. Silently, he preceded me back to the ranch house, where women obviously ruled. Within a few moments of our return he withdrew himself, his wife, and formerly available daughter to a private conference, leaving me to sweat it out on a heavy old tufted couch decorated with Indian blankets while nervously thumbing through a book on the history of cattle brands.

That the father had effectively spread the alarm of my moral ruin was apparent through the noon meal in the mother's chilly aloofness and in the daughter's stricken, outraged glances. Through the longest evening since Creation, the family father pointedly ignored me in favor of gut-thumping country tunes piped in over the radio. The family mother hovered protectively near Carol Jane, who was herself regally perched atop a private iceberg. This night knew no tender kisses, financial reports, or peeks at the family album.

On the Sabbath morn I lazed in bed, pleading a headache when the family departed for church. Hardly had their dust disappeared than I composed a short note equally touching on thanks for their hospitality and regret that some forgotten but vital obligation dictated my early return to Lubbock. In my haste to cover the mile to the highway and thumb a ride to safety, I neglected to claim the small canvas bag with its toilet articles and spare clothes I had hauled up from Texas Tech in Carol Jane's old Dodge. For years I wondered what disposition the disillusioned ranch family made of my abandoned clothing, though it now occurs to me they probably conducted a ceremonial burning.

Among the budding engineers, geologists, ranchers, school teachers, shop keepers, football coaches, and insurance agents I knew at Texas Tech were many young veterans of the military. Some few had served with black soldiers, as I had, though they had managed better to preserve their original racial attitudes. There were endless stories of how one "dumb nigger" or "big black buck" or another had screwed up a white-glove inspection so that an entire company had been unjustly punished for his slothful ways, or yarns of how some black GI had threatened a superior with multiple stab wounds. Certain imaginative old soldiers invented stories of how, motivated by the highest principles, they had successfully refused to salute black officers. Other than for my fellow scholars who remembered the indignities of integrated military units, none remarked in any way on the "Negro problem." Indeed, I recall absolutely no conversations touching on politics, social reform, history, literature, or sociology. Most of the small-town saplings and farm or ranch boys who shared life in Drane Hall talked almost exclusively of their career ambitions, football, sex, or cars.

On New Year's Day, I drew a seat in the Sun Bowl at El Paso near three former Texas Tech football players on hand to watch their old school try College of Pacific. The California school's star was Eddie Macon, a lithe and speedy black man named to several All-American teams. The ex–Red Raiders could hardly contain themselves while waiting for "Ole Gerald and Ole Red to lay that jitter-buggin' jig out," as one of the less subtle old grads promised everyone within earshot. Indeed, when Macon carried the ball on the initial play, he was laid low behind the scrimmage line. Great approving roars and whoops stirred Tech partisans: normal enough. What was perhaps less than normal was the number of persons who cried, "Kill that black ape," or other racist exhortations.

Late in the game, with Texas Tech two touchdowns ahead and obviously in control, the same fans cheered Eddie Macon for his fine play, which included a long touchdown run. My thought was one that I wouldn't have had even three years earlier: that all their cheers could not erase the original ugliness. Though my racial experiences in the Army and in the East had been less complete than I then presumed, exposure to black people at least had taught me that they had minds, dreams, and hurts like the rest of us, and in no way deserved their automatic exclusion. It wasn't so much seeing the black citizen without social or economic opportunity, or confined to his slums and inferior schools—though, God knows, these were major causes of our terrible social impasse. No, it was the million mindless "little" humiliations that stirred my tardy rage and soon caused me to be looked on as a little crazy and unreliable.

Texas Tech and I discovered a mutual disenchantment early on: I failed to put the anticipated muscle into its football squad, and its academic instructions did not promptly inspire my head to satisfying knowledge. Before the first semester ended I was cutting more classes than prevailing rules allowed, remaining in Drane Hall to stare out the windows across the windy Western landscape, pining for the lost excitements and promises of New York as the more rational might pine over the loss of a particularly talented mistress. In my room I composed several of the world's most hopeless short stories, and sent unanswered letters announcing my availibility as a star reporter to the *New York Times.* Having offered myself in vain to all Manhattan journals, I gave the Brooklyn *Eagle,* the Long Island *Press,* and even the Newark *Star-Ledger* their missed opportunities. As my true worth in Eastern newspaper circles began to register, I lowered my sights to include the Forth Worth *Star-Telegram,* Dallas *Morning News* and—yes!—the Amarillo *Globe-News,* of which I had been so contemptuous in Carol Jane's hay barn. Only the *Star-Telegram* responded, the editor saying that he had no current openings—then, curiously, suggesting that I apply to his newspaper's local competition, the Fort Worth *Press.* This so depleted my confidence that I sent no more applications.

Midway through the second semester, I abandoned even the pretense of attending classes. There followed dull days of drugged sleep, dominoes, and purposeless space-gazing; once, in honest desperation, I may have read a half-dozen pages in my History 101 text. Multiple requests from the Dean of Men that I drop by his office for curative chats were blithely ignored. More and more I found myself gravitating to a group of discouraged ex-GIs who lived for the arrival of their monthly government checks, promptly blowing them on bootleg whiskey, pinball machines, and bad poker judgments. One morning, not bothering to formally check out of school, I packed my dirty duds and hit the highway—drifting, purposeless as the native tumbleweeds. Dumped out of an oil truck in a small New Mexico town, I happened on a window sign proclaiming REPORTER WANTED (much as a quick-fry restaurant might solicit its waitresses) and, simply by inventing out of whole cloth a background as a reporter on papers in Long Branch and Red Bank in New Jersey, I landed the job. Except for having contributed an occasional article to the weekly newspaper at the Signal Corps Photo Center, and for telephoning in our post football and basketball résumés to the Long Island *Star-Journal,* I had not one single qualification.

I worked on that incredibly inferior publication for five months as its only reporter. The *Daily Sunshine,* we shall call it out of a warped sense of humor, was owned by a wealthy old woman in love with Old Guard Republicanism and reporters who cheerfully worked for $37.50 per week. When I asked for a raise to $50, the Old Guard's sweetheart ushered me to the back shop to exhibit a happy example from among the contented proletariat: Mose, an ancient Negro, operated our old flat-bed press, nursing it through daily breakdowns with kicks, thumps bailing wire, and Biblical exhortations. He also delivered our shoddy product to newsstands in an old pickup truck, hawked papers on street corners should we turn up a few newsboys short (as we often did, the newsboys never knowing if we might come within three hours of our scheduled press run), and generally applied his handy thumb wherever the dam sprang sudden leaks. "Mose has been with me for years," the old lady publisher screeched above the whines and groans of the antiquated back shop, "and *he* don't make fifty dollars a week! Why, you're making as much as he makes. You young boys come in here with thirty-five cents in your pocket and expect to strike it rich the first day." Mose was in that moment angrily kicking at the malfunctioning old press, having failed in his efforts to reason with it in the name of Jesus. I had seen the hovel he lived in across the tracks in "Harlem Heights" and knew that he struggled to assist a grandson or two trying to stay in high school. I did not, therefore, find the publishing lady's peculiar pitch inspirational in the cause of tenure. Within the hour I was back on the road to Texas, a minor-league Jack Kerouac, my thumb begging rides of lumbering oil tankers, cattle trucks, and whizzing sedans.

After two days as a telephone company lineman-trainee, I

discovered an unexpected talent for acrophobia. For a few weeks I burdened a drive-in restaurant as the most incompetent counterman ever to send out chicken-in-a-basket when the customer had clearly expressed a preference for hot dogs or fried shrimp; one day I dumped enough chocolate syrup into a container previously reserved for other liquids to give a bad name to our strawberry floats. This inspired my employer to proclaim his devout belief that not everyone was cut out for the food business, and to back his philosophy with a week's severance pay. The war being long over and manpower plentiful, no West Texas post office needed a former summer letter-carrier. My low point in this period came when, in the middle of country proud of its cattle heritage, I sold out briefly as a shoveler of goat droppings.

I resumed my old habit of writing letters begging affiliation with Texas newspapers. One morning in the fall of 1950 came a telephone call magically offering a job on a small daily in a town of approximately twenty thousand and located in the region where I had attended high school. The newspaper's one-man sports department had been recalled by the Air Force due to trouble in Korea, and did I want his old job? I wanted it even at a mere $55 per week, with no provisions to be paid for the required overtime. Over the next four years I would labor for that newspaper, for another one twenty miles away, and for a West Texas radio station so powerful it could be heard in the next county.

Working on that first sports desk, I ordered photographs of the Negro high-school basketball team—only to be instructed that our paper's policy precluded publication of "nigger art." (And, it developed, wedding or engagement announcements, or anything the black citizen involved himself in except crime or violent death.) For years the newspaper ignored the black community's plea that "Negro" be capitalized in print.

A Cuban-born baseball player for the local Longhorn League entry, dark enough to invite speculation, might be cheered for pitching a two-hitter, but an hour later he might be refused service at local restaurants specializing in ptomaine. Indeed, when the first Cuban had been signed for the local team, angry fans pledged to boycott its games. A year or two earlier, my predecessor in the sports slot had encouraged fans to mutiny against Cuban athletes' being added to the local roster on the dubious grounds "the foreigners" might somehow prevent "your son or mine" from misplaying a $200-per-month second baseman's job. After I sneaked a column into the newspaper favoring the employment of Cuban players, provided they possessed those minimal skills required for Class D baseball, not only many fans but my superiors on the newspaper were outraged.

The coach of our high-school football team asked that I prepare the way for the school's first Mexican-American varsity athlete through a story stressing the young man's excellent manners, scholastic worth, humility, and all-around ability. In an interview, the nervous young man slipped but once: "I washed dishes in this restaurant," he said—naming an establishment owned by a man prone to advertise his civic contributions—"but I can't eat there unless I eat in the kitchen. One time I went in there with some friends on my day off, and the boss said he was sorry but he couldn't serve us." That little gem was promptly blue-penciled by an agitated editor, an incredibly tiny man who, in compensation, affected the deep tones of Vaughan Monroe, and who was known behind his back as "Peahead" in tribute to his intellectual abilities. "Peahead" was always pointing out to visitors with some perverted pride that the President of the Negro Chamber of Commerce, who appeared reasonably bright and articulate, served our paper as its janitor and backshop handy man.

When I accompanied policemen in their patrol cars in my later role as police reporter, I was almost certain to see some Negro hailed as "Hey, Boy!" and forced to stand respectfully with a flashlight beam in his eyes while explaining where he was going on the public street. Though oilfield workers and ranch hands might brawl with beer bottles or knives in their hillbilly music emporiums, police responded only when carnage prompted the worried owners to call for assistance. In black clubs, however, police were always present: circling the dance floor, hard-eying the customers, checking for liquor violations or concealed weapons. On slow nights, when traffic patrol or station-house duty failed to excite, it was routine to hear officers say, "Let's go bust us a few jigs."

Everyone in town knew of a certain posh gambling house near the Country Club where our white high-rollers knew not to expect the sheriff unless he happened by to solicit their votes; a similar sense of security could be found among those improving themselves at card tables on the eighth floor of our leading hotel, where the sign on the door advertised "Athletic Club." You could read in our newspaper, however, of raids by our alert lawmen on two-bit dice games involving straying citizens with unimpressive addresses and names like Willie Washington, Roosevelt (Doglegs) Jackson, or Jesus Gonzalez. "If you didn't have a white captain in the old days," Louis Armstrong told me over bourbon one night in the summer of 1967, "you was just a damn sad nigger. If a Negro had a proper white man to reach the law and say, 'What the hell you mean locking up *my* nigger?' then—quite naturally—the law would walk him free. Get in that jail *without* your white boss, and yonder comes the chain gang!" The old jazz king may not have been as instructional as he presumed: I had frequently, in "the old days" of the 1950s, seen the Willie Washingtons or Jesus Gonzalezes "walked free" or given wrist-tapping fines because they had the good luck to mow the proper white man's lawn or a wife who attended the kitchens or children of good white families; the Roosevelt (Doglegs) Jacksons, in the absence of viable connections, might find themselves doing sixty to ninety days for "gaming." When a former city councilman and member of the school board, who owned our largest appliance store, had the misfortune to be driving a Cadillac that suddenly jumped a curb, sheared off a couple of parking meters, and crashed into the window display of a local department store at a suspicious hour, my publisher came around to announce the event as being unworthy of reporting in our paper—settlements had been made all around, George was a good old boy who just happened to have a bit of bad luck and, besides, he had been driving under the influence of medication prescribed for some unspecified illness. When a half-dozen black fry cooks and shine boys were arrested for possession of a paltry amount of marijuana, however, we sent photographers and reporters along with the raiding party, then splashed the big "dope raid" across the front page in Second Coming type.

Rocky, a city detective who claimed as an Infantryman once to have lipped back at General Patton was especially feared by blacks. A towering, large-boned man, he had a hatred for "thugs and thieves" that may have been psychotic, and his morals could be so outraged by the sight of pimps or dice artists that he might beat them half senseless as the first step in their reform. When Rocky strutted into one of the black clubs, his lower lip curling and nostrils dilated as if sniffing fumes from the city sewage works, his thumping cowboy boots intimidating the wooden floors, the smarter customers sat tight and quiet. They were careful to answer in respectful tones even if addressed as "Nigger," "Boy," or "You black bastard." One night Rocky parked his car in front of a club he rated as especially troublesome, then sneaked by a circular route into a rear entrance. A Negro man sitting with his back to the detective apparently heard someone warn that the feared lawman's car was parked out front. "Motherfuck the goddamn laws," the black man said (as witnesses later would attest). "I ain't studying no goddamn laws." He was launching into a description of how "the laws" would fare badly should they mess with his bad ass, when Rocky's big fist crashed on the back of his neck. The black man was hauled off to jail on a charge of "resisting arrest"—a neat feat for an unconscious man who never even caught a glimpse of the arresting officer.

Persistent reports reached me that Rocky had awarded brutal beatings, including one to a white girl visiting from California, whose misfortune it was to be caught in bed with a local black man. None of these stories could be tied down sufficiently for publication (for, as I had learned, my publisher demanded airtight cases before risking the wilder truths). It was almost impossible to find witnesses, or even victims, willing to talk. I had seen enough of Rocky's enthusiastic use of violence in making even routine arrests, however, and knew enough of his righteous attitudes, to judge him less than blameless. Once he carelessly bragged of having "broken in" his new blackjack on a smart-mouthed drunk nigger. When I demanded an investigation from the Chief of Police (known in the community for his excellence at playing "Mister Interlocutor" in the annual black-face minstrel show performed by the Downtown Lions Club), Rocky quickly changed his story: Naw, he hadn't hit nobody; why, goddammit, he hadn't said no such a-thing. And, hellfire, if he *had* said it he had only been a-joking. End of investigation.

Some years later, after Rocky had departed town in pursuit of other culprits, and I was no longer a newsman but a Congressional assistant visiting old friends, a former detective who had worked with Rocky admitted that my original suspicions had been correct. "The FBI investigated ole Rocky for abusing prisoners half a dozen times," he claimed. "They never filed formal charges, but they *did* warn him he was on dangerous ground. And a couple of times they even persuaded the Chief to chew his butt out."

If Rocky deserved distinction as the police-department heavy, Red was its undisputed good guy. A cheerful, orange-haired little man with something of Red Skelton in his mug and manner, he actually read books and sometimes intelligently discussed them; soon he became my natural favorite among West Texas lawmen. Late one Thanksgiving Eve I accompanied Red at his invitation to several homes in the Negro section, where he delivered gift baskets of turkey and all the trimmings. Red was warmly greeted by the women of the houses, and by young tots who roused themselves from sleep the moment their antennae picked up the approach of excitement. (The man of the house, I noted, was rarely present; when he was, he seemed almost pathetically ill at ease.) These were pitiful hovels we called on, truly miserable places, the wind blowing through cracks in their plank walls, magazine photos of movie stars pasted up as incongruous decorations: it somehow seemed insane that Tyrone Power or Joan Blondell grinned from their white, well-fed, putty faces in such dark and cheerless surroundings. The only heating generally was supplied by wood-burning stoves or open-flame gas heaters; virtually none of the shacks boasted electricity or even bathrooms. Often three or four children slept to a bed. (On the first of each month, remember, our papers routinely bannered stories proclaiming local bank deposits to be at record highs, and no Chamber of Commerce press release or after-dinner speaker failed to cite our remarkable prosperity as the perfect example of what Free Enterprise could do if only men would get off their duffs and dig for gold or strike oil as God intended.)

"You cute little bugger," Red shouted in scooping up small black children, whirling them around and around to their obvious delight; their mothers or grandmothers beamed, God-blessing "Mistah Red" for his exceptional heart. Back in the car, Red grew expansive: Why, he didn't have anything against Nigras; matter of fact, he liked 'em; he felt sorry for the poor devils; you wouldn't see *him* giving Nigras a hard time like some other badge-toters he could name.

I was so touched by Red's unusual philanthrophy as to suggest writing a feature story about it. Red became adamant against the idea, near desperately so. Policemen, I had learned, lusted after favorable publicity no less than did politicians or beauty-contest winners. Why, then, couldn't I write about Red's exceptional charity? Red said a bit lamely that, well, he didn't want any credit for a private deal, or the police chief (who dearly loved a good headline himself) might grow envious of Red's publicity, or Red's fellow officers might be angered. He would be embarrassed at best, probably castigated. "For God's sakes," he admonished, "don't even let on to the Chief that I brought you with me."

By now suspicious, I engaged in private snooping: Red's largesse did not spring directly from his own pocket, it developed, but from a special police-department fund. And his philanthropic errands extended only to those few needy families who had proved themselves "reliable informants"—i.e., efficient stool pigeons against their black brothers or sisters, the better to provide "law and order." So much for the good guys.

Another "good guy" soon disappointed me. He was a cheerful young officer employed by the Texas Highway Patrol. I rejoiced when he announced for sheriff against an incumbent gun-toter particularly odious to me. The old incumbent, who for years had ruled as if by right of blood line, enforced the law best against those who had little or no political clout; he kept the sorriest bunch of deputies since Goebbels. One day I encouraged the young challenger to campaign among black voters —even, if necessary, surreptitiously, so as not to alienate the white majority. Surely local blacks were secret enemies of the oppressive sheriff; given even the smallest private encouragement they might vote in record numbers. "Well, naw," my white hope said. "The way I figger it, half the niggers will vote for me by mistake even if a-tryin' to vote for the other feller. You try to tell niggers *how* to vote, and it'll just confuse 'em."

One heard from law-enforcement sources how very violent the black man was by nature. And, indeed, though we were in country where so much of the old frontier spirit remained that white men often settled with guns those disputes more properly the jurisdiction of our courts, there probably *were* proportionally more incidents among Negroes of murder, aggravated assault, and incidental Saturday-night bashings. Often, riding with the cops in search of news scoops, I was a witness to savage street brawls and artful knifings in the black district; more than once I was in the presence of a black body from which the life had just bled into the West Texas dust. (One night I followed the remains of a murdered black man through its grisly attentions by morticians; they relieved the strain by making a series of cracks relating to the late citizen's sex parts, then by branching off into nigger jokes.) A scheme to control unruly blacks by hiring a few Negro policemen (these being carefully instructed never to attempt arrests on white people, their authority extending only to the black ghetto) backfired because black officers were discovered to possess quicker trigger fingers than did their white counterparts. "A white law will beat your ass," the wise dudes said in the local Flats, "but a colored law might shoot you."

(Years later, Eldridge Cleaver would offer his explanation of the phenomenon: "A glance through any black newspaper will prove that black people in America kill each other with regularity. This is the internalized violence of oppressed people. Angered by the misery of their lives but cowed by the over superior might of the oppressor, the oppressed people shrink from striking out at the true objects of their hostility and strike instead at their more defenseless brothers and sisters near at hand. Somehow this seems safer, less fraught with dire consequences, as though one is less dead when shot down by one's brother than when shot down by one's oppressor. It is merely criminal to take up arms against one's brother, but to step outside the vicious circle of the internalized violence of the oppressed and take up arms against the oppressor is to step outside of life itself, to step outside of the structure of this world, to enter, almost alone, the no-man's land of revolution.")

Prosecutors in our courts complained because they couldn't get jurors excited by "nigger killings." "Hell," the familiar recital went, "you spend the state's time and money convicting one nigger of killing another nigger and he likely won't get more than three to five years—and half the time the damned jury will recommend a suspended sentence." Nothing better demonstrated that small value white jurors placed on black lives. Conversely, a black man who had burglarized, robbed, or otherwise offended white values could rarely count on justice tempered with mercy.

Any black man called for jury duty was excused from service on one ground or another—once the lawyers, and possibly the judge, had properly enjoyed him: "You the same Willie Johnson who beats his wife and works as a bellhop over at the hotel selling bootleg liquor?" Condescending chuckles would sweep the courtroom while the poor black man struggled with so impossible a question.

I went to my editor with a suggestion that we run a series on double standards in our courts, police operations, hospitals, and other public institutions. He tried to laugh the subject away, but ultimately said he would speak to the publisher. Weeks passed. When I brought up the topic again, the editor told me to write a sample of what I had in mind. I delivered a well-documented story, and promptly heard no more. One night when we shared more drinks than was good for secrets, I raised the sore subject again. "Look," he said, "stop spinning your wheels. The publisher hit the ceiling when I mentioned your goddamned nigger series. If I turned in that story you wrote he'd probably fire us both."

Dammit, I said, the obligation of a newspaper was to publish the facts.

My editor, who had already served on a half dozen newspapers without being hurt in any big crusades, grinned cynically. "The duty of *this* newspaper," he said, "is to make money and boost the town and confine our muckraking to bitching about taxes. I understood that when I took my job."

An old friend had become addicted to a Fundamentalist brand of religion. Each beer I drank, each weak oath I muttered, each awkward cowboy waltz my legs attempted at roadside honky-tonks brought dire predictions of the temperatures my soul would know through eternity's long and parching night. One day he invited me to attend a black Sunday-school class he taught on alternate Sundays: he had headed a drive of his sect to establish a church of the Faith among Negroes. Well, I thought, perhaps some good has come from his crazed commitments. Maybe he would get to know the black person as an individual, not merely as somebody to mow his lawn or accomplish his wife's ironing.

How long had he taught the black class?

Oh, for almost a year.

And how did he approach the task?

He sprang to a small blackboard in his study and began to draw crude pictures to illustrate Creation as reported in Genesis: the sun to represent light, stick figures representing Adam and Eve, and so on. His art was accompanied by Dick-and-Jane prattle to explain the language of the Bible.

"Do you think all that primitive art is necessary?" I asked my Christian friend.

"Oh, sure." He laughed. "Those niggers eat it up. You got to put on a show to keep their attention. They're just like a bunch of little children . . . or monkeys."

My father was working on a construction job; one night he told me how much fun the crew had out of "Nigger James."

"He's a purty good ole nigger," Dad said of the black man hired to step-and-fetch for carpenters, plumbers, and other craftsmen. "He don't hardly ever get mad, though we guy and hoo-raw him a right smart." He told how one of the white carpenters had asked, "Why all you black boys have such terrible smells?" James had finally agreed, under duress, that perhaps black people were not as inherently sanitary as whites. "If you don't take more baths," the white bully instructed, "we're gonna give you a GI bath on payday." James reportedly laughed, perhaps nervously, in promising to mind his sanitation. On payday, the fastidious carpenter filled a barrel with cold water, provided strong soaps, and invited his companions to help scrub James down.

Though my father had not participated in the scrubbing, he was almost helpless with laughter in recounting the scene. "You ought to a-seen that nigger fight and squawl. Lord God, you would a-thought they was tryin' to electrocute him. They throwed him in that barrel, clothes and all, and scrubbed him awhile and then let him go. He taken it so well they made up a little collection and give him five dollars."

"Well, Jesus Christ!" I exploded. "How the hell else could he take it, without you peckerwoods hanging him?"

My father's face froze; he picked up his newspaper, crackling it angrily. When he had regained control he said, "They was just havin' a little fun. Nobody was tryin' to hurt him. You don't seem to know the difference."

Shortly after the Supreme Court had shocked the South by ordering public schools desegregated in May of 1954, I attended that old institution, the family reunion, famed for its nostalgic stories, covered-dish feasts, and cousins largely remembered as foes in ancient rubber-gun fights. We were at Uncle Earl's house, in Putnam, and, following a rich heavy luncheon delightfully served by a covey of nice old aunts ("Now, Lawrence, you not only been ignoring my pickled peaches, you haven't ate a bite of your Aunt Ethel's devil's food cake"), I had slipped away for a nap. Awakening, I heard my father in an adjoining parlor discussing current events with Uncle Earl and Uncle John.

"The trouble is," Dad was saying, "nobody don't seem to give a durn."

"Naw," Uncle John said. "They don't care. Especially the young people."

"My own boy," Dad said. "He's got it in his head a nigger's good as a white man."

"You can't do much to change 'em, either," Uncle Earl said. "They laugh at you."

"Or get mad," Dad said.

There was a silence while the old men rocked and digested their fried chicken and thought their melancholy thoughts, possibly wondering at the purpose heaven had in mind when it had so tricked their sons.

"Well," Uncle John said after the long pause, "I guess it's good it didn't happen in our day."

"Yeah," Uncle Earl agreed. "I just hate to think what our

grandchildren have to go through." Though I then had no way of knowing it (having held no stop watches on "all deliberate speed"), many of those grandchildren, then toddlers, would complete high school before their schools would experience even token integration.

In 1954 I was a reporter in a Texas town of some fifty thousand, made newly prosperous by oil. For many of our citizens the Great Depression remained green in the memory, a nightmare of day-before-yesterday that had deprived them of educations, decent wages, even enough food to eat. Some had new homes, new cars, and community status for the first time. Wanting nothing in their good lives changed, they reacted violently to all presumed socio-political threats. Senator Joe McCarthy's witch-hunting tactics were popular in the extreme, so much so that when I wrote a sympathetic story of Corporal Claude Batchelor's return to the small west Texas town from which he had marched off to Korea (there to become one of twenty-one American GIs who for a time refused repatriation to the United States during prisoner exchanges at Panmunjom), our ultra-conservative newspaper became the target of nuts and kooks who saw a Communist plot in our reporting such "Red" news. I felt sorry for Batchelor. A high-school dropout who came from a large family in the meanest economic circumstances, he was captured when barely eighteen years old. "They pointed out how this rich country has neglected its poor people," Batchelor said of his "brainwashing" captors, "and especially its Negro people. I thought about what I had seen back here, and decided it was true."

The Supreme Court's school desegregation decision hit town like a thunderclap. Stopping for coffee on my daily reporter's rounds I found businessmen, lawyers, oil-company employees, and local politicos getting their heads together in steamy plots to circumvent the new ruling. Though "niggers in our schools" was on all tongues, our newspaper moguls decided the less said in print the better: maybe the problem would somehow dry up and blow away.

Later in the summer, however, I heard rumors that a black man planned to enroll in the local junior college come September. It was no snap to track him down in the Negro section, where citizens were naturally suspicious of any white man anxious to locate one of their brothers: the outsider might be a policeman, a bill collector, a lawyer, or otherwise the bearer of traditional bad tidings. The search was further complicated by my role as a newsman frequently seen in the company of the hated police. Eventually, with the aid of a paid police informant, I learned the young black man's name and found him in his parent's small frame house. He was reading Mickey Spillane to a background of what we whites then called "race records," now popularly known as soul music.

Willie Byrd, we shall call him, was very black and less than enthusiastic. "Well, yeah," he admitted, "I plan on enrolling out there. The big court says I can."

Did he anticipate trouble?

"No, I think people will obey the law. And the law says I can attend college where I want. Some of the older people, you know, they may snort and fuss. But I think young people are pretty level-headed these days."

Had he previously attended integrated schools?

"No, I went to high school here. Then I was in the Army two years. Last year I attended this Negro college down in Houston for one term. It cost so much staying away from home, see, and I just had a part-time job washing cars, so I had to quit."

Why did he want to be the first black in the local college?

"That's not it. Nobody's backing me in this thing. It's a matter of money. This is my home and I can attend college here cheaper than anywhere else, 'cause I can sleep and eat at home."

Had he experienced social contacts with whites?

"Well, I was in the Army with white fellows. We never had no trouble to speak of. Some white fellows was pretty friendly."

Then the young black man exposed the depth of his naïveté:

"Say, now, I wasn't counting on big headlines. I just hoped to go out there and enroll without any fuss. Now here *you* are, and this morning I got a telegram from one of the big television stations in Dallas wanting to come out here and make films. Some of my people, you know, they think this thing might work out better if it can be kept out of the spotlight."

Forget it, I said; he was now a symbolic figure and, therefore, public property.

Our newspaper displayed the Willie Byrd interview on page one of its Sunday edition, along with a photograph of the would-be scholar stiffly posed in his best suit. On Monday, as I made my police-beat rounds, a deputy sheriff, who always seemed to have last shaved about three days before, accosted me in the courthouse. "Boy," he said, "I seen where you give that damn nigger plenty of ink in yesterday's paper. Wellsir, I got something to show you about that blackbird." He whipped out his billfold, removing a carbon copy of an arrest sheet: "See, we got him on charges of carrying a concealed weapon. That's the kinda sumbitch you're writing up on the front page, and that's the kinda sumbitch that N-Double-A-Sea-Pea outfit always picks to make trouble. They're paying that blackbird five thousand dollars and costs to bust into our college."

Where had the deputy received his information?

"Hell far!" he snorted. *"Everybody* knows he was paid to make trouble. That's all people been talking about."

Though the arrest sheet revealed no final disposition of the case, and failed to specify the weapon allegedly concealed, the deputy swore that the black man "done ninety days." A check of court records, however, proved the charges had been dismissed. Willie Byrd had not been convicted of anything.

The grizzled old Justice of the Peace, known to lend money at rates of usury and to be the absentee landlord of several miserable "nigger shacks," could recall nothing of the specifics. He was, for a fact, a borderline illiterate. This, combined with his native cunning, caused him to keep such careless books and to tell such casually contradictory stories that a newspaper team investigating him for fraud had finally quit the task as hopeless; he simply didn't keep enough records, or remember enough, to incriminate himself.

I sought Willie Byrd's version. Yes, he had been arrested while on Army furlough. Police had raided a black club, arresting everyone present because drinking had extended past the hour allowed by state law—a regulation invoked far more against black than white clubs. Raiding officers had not been gentle, by Willie Byrd's account, cursing and slugging one of his pals on finding a pistol in his possession. Willie Byrd admitted that while in the Army he had vowed to remain silent no longer when maltreated by whites, or when he saw other blacks maltreated, and so he had protested. For his pains, he said, the officers had charged him with possession of the weapon actually belonging to his friend. Willie Byrd's father, working through his white boss, who had convinced the old J.P. that too much contradictory evidence existed to support a conviction, had gotten the charge dropped.

Shortly after I talked with him about that old case, Willie Byrd was arrested on drunk-and-disorderly charges, fined in J.P. Court, and released. The jubilant old deputy brought this information on the following morning: "We caught your college-boy nigger drunk in one of them joints, and he tried to give us a buncha shit and resisted arrest." Willie Byrd was now not only discouraged, he was hostile: "Man, I was in this place eating supper and drinking beer with it. These officers come in and said, 'Boy, how much you been drinking?' I said I was on my second beer. One of 'em said, 'Git up and walk me a straight line, Boy.' I said, 'What have I done? Who am I bothering, man? I'm twenty-one.' I stood up from the counter and one of these officers lunged into me, bumped me back into the counter, and then he smiled real shitty and said, 'Boy, you done *resisted* me.' Man, they had me out in that police car before I knew what was happening. Locked my arms around behind me and handcuffed me. On the way to jail they joked about teaching me things I couldn't learn in college."

The arresting officers, who had not informed Willie Byrd that he might request a blood test to determine his degree of intoxication, if any, swore that he had been ass-grabbing drunk, had cursed them without provocation as they entered on "routine patrol," and "took a swing" at one of the three armed deputies. Black witnesses were found who verified Willie Byrd's version: they had not been present at his quick night trial, however, since officers had assured them his case would not be called until the following day. Normally, that would have been correct information: persons charged with intoxication were not customarily tried until several sobering hours had elapsed.

The old J.P., who had fined Willie Byrd in excess of $100 and costs, claimed only to have accommodated him with a midnight hearing following intervention by the white man for whom the elder Mr. Byrd worked. "They just wanted to get it over with so the nigger boy wouldn't have to spend the night in jail." Willie Byrd disagreed: his father's white boss had telephoned only to guarantee the posting of prompt bail. Instead of releasing him on bail, however, arresting officers had immediately rushed Willie Byrd into J.P. Court to attain a rapid conviction. "It was my word against three officers," he said. "I didn't have lawyers, witnesses, nothing. That judge told me, 'You want to pay your fine and go on home, or plead not guilty and lay around in jail until your trial?' That jail's no place to lay around, man. I paid my fine and shucked on out of there." *

I went to an FBI agent, told him the story, and requested an investigation. "Will he sign a complaint?" he asked. No, Willie Byrd didn't want additional trouble or attention. "My hands are tied unless he's willing to make an official complaint." On my police rounds, where I was rapidly becoming as popular as Typhoid Mary, word soon circulated of my attempting to call the FBI's wrath down in behalf of "that damn nigger." *I* had not

* The white boss in question refused to discuss the matter with newsmen on the grounds that "I've got to live in this town and do business in it. Get me involved in a nigger crusade, and you've got a lawsuit."

told anyone, because my editor had strongly advised against my approaching the FBI on the grounds it might make police-department relations more difficult for the newspaper.

Only a few days before Willie Byrd would presumably present himself for enrollment, he was arrested on a felony charge —attempted rape. No arrest record was immediately filed on the public record, however; no deputy came running to spread the news. I would not learn of the charge until the accused black man had been freed on posting a sizable bond—and had disappeared. "Willie saw the handwriting on the wall," his father said. "Trouble was waiting for him 'round every corner. I doubt he'll be back. Long as he don't come back, I'm satisfied they won't call him for trial. And please, don't stir things up by writing about him again in your newspaper." He was a tall, thin man of careful pride, but on that morning as he talked to me in his small frame house, nervous and chain-smoking, he obviously was frightened and defeated.

The young black woman who had filed the charge proved reluctant: the "laws," she said, had advised her against talking to newspaper people. She would say only that Willie Byrd had come to her home while her parents were away, had "got fresh with me" and then had slapped and threatened her when she wouldn't submit. Yes, she had dated Willie Byrd a time or two. Yes, he had visited her home several times. No, he had never before mistreated her, though they had had "a few spats." No, nobody had influenced her except her mother, who had insisted she go to the courthouse to place Willie Byrd under a peace bond forbidding his harassments. The mother, however, volunteered that at the courthouse a "law" convinced them that rather than seeking a peace bond the young woman should file charges of attempted rape.

Willie Byrd did not present himself for enrollment at the local college. To the best of my knowledge, he did not return to town. The attempted rape charge was never presented to a grand jury for action; all charges were ultimately dropped at the request of the complaining witness.

I cannot attest, for a certainity, how blameless Willie Byrd was in these various matters. I can attest, however, that lawmen developed a quick and unusual interest in his future from the moment his educational plans became known. I also recall how they enjoyed baiting me about the troubles of "your college nigger," and certainly I had seen enough of the way blacks were treated at the hands of "law and order" agents that any claim he made might be assumed potentially true. There seems little doubt as to how those old events were interpreted in the Flats: not for several years more would another black student petition the local college.

I do not recall that our politicians seriously began to holler "nigger" in my home precincts until the mid-1950s. There was little purpose in such exercises earlier, since we whites so obviously held the power reins. Even our most flagrant acts of discrimination had gone unchallenged for so long that most citizens never considered the prospect of change. True, we had heard from a disgruntled few when the white man's primary had been knocked down as unconstitutional, but that had somehow seemed remote and unreal in my West Texas village. One remembers, too, some rantings against Harry Truman's antilynch legislation (which Lyndon B. Johnson voted against, as did our other Texas congressmen and senators to a man) and brayings against the Fair Employment Practice Committee established in Washington. And while some of our prominent citzens, enraged by Hubert Humphrey's fiery civil-rights speech at the Democratic National Convention in 1948, had bolted to Strom Thurmond's Dixiecrats, Harry Truman had carried the day in Texas after being endorsed by Governor Beauford Jester and most of our working politicos—possibly because HST did not once mention civil rights or anti-lynch laws or FEPC while campaigning in Texas that year. Resentments built, however, as the Supreme Court ordered the University of Texas to provide for blacks in its law school. But it was the 1954 decision on desegregation of public schools that caused race to become a growing factor in our political campaigns.

Our newspapers and statesmen jointly predicted that civil rights laws would be drawn as the foundation stones for establishing a Gestapo-like federal police force sure to knock on our doors at the first midnight opportunity. FEPC laws would bankrupt business and leave commerce in chaos as unskilled workers were elevated to positions beyond their natural capacities, and, furthermore, would deprive businessmen of their God-given right to hire the employees of their choice. Men of alien isms worked like worms in the rotten carcass of the federal structure, determined to redesign our social machinery along lines pleasing to Moscow: hadn't Joe McCarthy, Richard Nixon, Strom Thurmond said so?

These pleadings were especially effective in Texas, perhaps the most chauvinistic of states, where a new wealth was superimposing itself over the old Populist notions of an earlier time. As Texas had once enjoyed the status of an independent republic with its own President and Congress, its own home-grown heroes at the Alamo and San Jacinto, there was the presumption (greatly reinforced by the mandatory teaching of a glowing Texas history in the public schools) of a natural superiority in our way of doing things. And there was the corollary suspicion, often affirmed by our politicians, that "outsiders" schemed around the clock to bring us down to their own low levels through the uses of oppressive laws and naked power. As Texas had cast its lot with the Confederacy against Lincoln and the Abolitionists, we tended to view federal authority with that bitter hostility the loser historically directs against his conqueror. As we had won our independence in blood-letting against Mexicans with darker skins than our own, we were doubly aroused against the federal force when it came preaching racial integration. Though the modern descendants of early-day pioneers might have long ago grown fat and effete compared with their forefathers who had tamed the Texas frontier with guns, plows, or cow ponies, they continued to pride themselves on retaining a hardy frontier spirit which precluded meddling in their affairs. Our most ambitious politicians were careful to pander to our darkest instincts, crying their praises of "our sacred state's rights" or condemnations against "outside agitators" at every opportunity. Everyone knew what they meant: keep the niggers in their place.

Governor Allan Shivers, cleverly mixing the menaces of Communism, labor bosses, and outside agitators, founded a dynasty on Texas fears. If the governor had not been so harassed by insidious influences working day and night to plant the hammer and sickle in Austin, he might have discerned scandals in the Veteran's Land Program, among the state's loosely chartered insurance firms, or among careless elements in the real-estate trade. As it turned out, a small weekly newspaper was left to discover these embarrassing shortcomings which robbed the taxpayers generally, defrauded many individuals, and made other persons suspiciously rich. Only after a prominent insurance tycoon chose suicide, another sought the better climate of Brazil, and prison terms were awarded to a state representative, a former state senator and the popular commissioner of public lands, did the Texas power structure take uneasy notice of rotten odors in Austin. Though the governor himself was never charged with wrongdoing, he did have the extraordinary good luck while in public office to buy a certain parcel of land for $25,000 and sell the same parcel seven months later for $450,000.

Governor Shivers had as his most serious opponent in the 1954 Democratic primary an Austin lawyer, former district judge, and ex-assistant state attorney general, Ralph Yarborough.* The Texas power structure suspected Judge Yarborough of peculiar governmental notions: his approach to rule hinged

---

* Yarborough was elected to the United States Senate three years later, in 1957, where he served until defeated in the 1970 Democratic primary by an opponent who made much of his votes against confirming Judges Haynsworth and Carswell to the United States Supreme Court.

on his belief that all citizens were entitled to participation in the democratic process. This so outraged our fearless press that only a handful of weekly newspapers, and the El Paso *Herald-Post* exclusively among dailies, endorsed Judge Yarborough. Most, in fact, merrily joined in indicting him. The challenger was tied to every unpopular group or cause his detractors could call to mind: labor bosses, outside agitators, alien sources in Washington, or worse. A number of secondary-school teachers and state-affiliated college instructors were flatly told that their attraction to the Yarborough candidacy made them unfit for promotion or, sometimes, even to retain their jobs. Small businessmen known to favor Judge Yarborough suddenly found their loans called by formerly friendly bankers. Congressmen and state legislators, to say nothing of eager young pols on the rise at the local level, were pressured to endorse Governor Shivers while defaming his primary detractor. Despite all these applied pressures, Judge Yarborough finished only twenty thousand votes behind the powerful incumbent in the first primary. Obviously, if he could attract a fair share of votes that had gone to other (and presumably anti-Shivers) candidates in the first primary, he might win. There was launched against Judge Yarborough a vicious and artful campaign. Unfortunately for his candidacy, the power structure had thirty additional days in which to arouse Texans against the Supreme Court's new school-desegregation decision.

Perhaps the most effective device was a statewide tour by alarmed "Citizens of Port Arthur," an industrial bog on the Gulf Coast. Port Arthur had become the focal point of a drive by labor unions (handicapped by repressive state laws) to organize Texas's growing army of industrial workers. Violence flared among labor organizers, company men, police, scabs, and union loyalists; Texas newspapers eagerly bannered news detrimental to the union cause, publishing over near the truss ads —if at all—reports of incidents where company hirelings, Texas Rangers, or other state officers, acting in the name of liberty, broke the heads of union sympathizers.

In the intense heat of the runoff election, rolling troupes fanned out across Texas to bring "The Port Arthur Story." That the handful of citizens who participated may not have accurately represented an entire city, or that all viewpoints in the labor-management dispute may not have been given fair airings, seemed lost on the Texas press. Headlines in most newspapers heralded the coming of the alarmed "Citizens of Port Arthur" in superlatives that surely would have caused advance agents for medicine shows, circuses, or faith healers to weep in gratitude.

I joined local citizens who jammed the ballroom of our most impressive hotel to hear the horrible tales. A young banker well-known as Governor Shivers' local campaign manager introduced our visitors: a wispy-voiced blond "housewife and mother," a minister with appropriately pious smiles, a corporate lawyer, three or four "small independent businessmen" with the solid look of stumpy oak trees, a couple of "distinguished civic leaders" who carried that natural air of confidence assumed by the ruling elite, and one palsied "early-day pioneer" dressed as if for leading a rodeo parade or for riding out to assist Custer. All were white—need it be said?—and not one appeared as underfed or as much a refugee from terror as their road-show billings indicated.

Oh, it was smooth. Smooth as satin, fine diamonds, babies' asses. I never saw anything to approach it for sheer *chutzpah,* corn, or effectiveness—though I would later spend ten years in the political major leagues, some in the company of LBJ, a fraction in the company of JFK. First the local Shivers manager compared our visitors to the Pilgrim Fathers in the matters of integrity, high principle, and fortitude, without the Pilgrim Fathers' taking a single match. The minister intimately talked over with God (in the presence of a mere three hundred witnesses) those special problems Texas faced, now beseeching, now scolding, now talking to Him as if He were an erring schoolboy and now as if He might have been a boyhood pal; by the time he finished, God had not a leg left to stand on—

assuming he was Christian and fair-minded. The sturdy businessmen recited their pieces about being driven to ruin by exorbitant union demands. One of the distinguished civic leaders described in outraged tones how the visiting parson (too good a man for heaven, the implication was) had been driven from his pulpit by union agents who, acting under orders from unspecified dark sources, had joined his congregation to spread damaging lies, rumors, dissent. The old "early-day pioneer" in a quavering voice remembered when men had been men in Texas: would they be again?

The *coup de grâce,* however, was reserved for the "housewife and mother." She was a petite lady, blue-eyed and blond. She spoke in soft Southern syllables sure to call up images of a gentle mother crooning her child to sleep, of the patient Sunday-school teacher impressing the words of "Jesus Loves Me" on her precious and tuneless young charges, of the tender and loving wife capable of turning into a lovely demon in the connubial bed. She was perfect for the role, and I have always wondered at their luck in finding her. With her fragile blonde construction and whispery tones one could easily imagine her snapped like a twig, broken, violated, crushed by dark forces. The director who cast her understood well the white man's preoccupation with that old fear-fantasy projecting something long and black and throbbing into milady's snow-white and sanctified drawers.

The lady whispered into a microphone of how she had escorted her young daughter to a Port Arthur shop to purchase "her junior-high-school graduation outfit." Pickets, "including several Nigras," had attempted to force their propagandizing handbills on her. She had politely refused, as a proper lady should, and had tried to move around the pickets into the store. They had shoved their faces almost against hers, had blocked her way and that of her child's, and when she asked them to please step aside they cursed her in the foulest possible terms. And one of the pickets had shouted that soon nobody would enter such blankety-blank scab stores, because there wouldn't *be* any terrible-obscenity scab stores. And a Nigra, now, had put his big ole face right up against hers and had shouted, *And that's because our man Yarborough gonna win!*

Gasps. Small wounded cries from the womenfolk. Angry mutterings from their men. Our good burghers quaked in righteous indignation; their white faces turned blood red at the public affirmation of everything they had believed deep in their bones and had known they would hear. After the local Shivers shill recovered his poise, he warned against certain bloc-voting precincts known for agitation, radicalism, general shiftlessness, and high crime rates. Results of the first gubernatorial primary, he stressed, revealed that such dangerous enclaves had voted ninety per cent or better on the side of America's enemies. It was the obvious duty of every right-thinking, independent-minded Texan to rush out and meet bloc-vote with bloc-vote. Among the enthusiastic I spotted our hardest-hitting ministers, better-connected bankers and oil czars, Chamber of Commerce pooh-bahs, city councilmen, policemen, school officials, and my own newspaper publisher.

My friend and lawyer Warren Burnett, who managed a number of west Texas counties for Judge Yarborough, gave his verdict: "They've put the big black britches on him. In that first primary, Ralph ran like Whirlaway. In the second one, he's gonna run like Old Dobbin." Sure enough, Governor Shivers carried by embarrassingly large margins almost all of Texas. That election would determine the course of race relations in Texas for years.

Two years later, Governor Shivers twice called out the Texas Rangers and the State Highway Patrol (first at Texarkana on the Arkansas-Texas border, and then at Mansfield, a rural village near Fort Worth) to prevent racial integration of the public schools. These remain the only incidents on record where a state government defied federal court desegregation orders by a show of force—and got away with it, clean. Orval Faubus didn't have that success, or George Wallace or Ross Barnett or Claude Kirk. Allan Shivers, establishing the example, did.

"Now, in the Texas case"—said President Eisenhower, speaking of the Mansfield incident at a press conference (after having first confessed ignorance of the specific details), "there was—the attorney for the students did report this violence and asked help, which apparently was the result of unreadiness to obey a federal court order. But before anyone could move, the Texas authorities had moved in and order was restored, so the question became unimportant."

Order of a sort *was* restored, though at the expense of the court order's being obeyed. President Eisenhower apparently thought it unimportant that he deal with the question of whether black children would be permitted to claim their citizens' rights. So, one must assume from the record, did Senate Majority Leader Lyndon B. Johnson, who proved not at all eager to discuss these successful acts of defiance in his home state. Soon the question became moot, thanks to Texas Attorney General John Ben Shepperd, who managed to poke legal holes in petitions filed on behalf of black students. Ultimately, in the absence of encouragement from Washington, the blacks gave up and their cause was swept unmourned under the soiled political rug.

These incidents occurred in 1956, however, and we must now backtrack two years by changing the scene to Washington.

# IV
# The Politician

"All respect we may have had for politicians, preachers, lawyers, governors, Presidents, senators, congressmen was utterly destroyed as we watched them temporizing and compromising over right and wrong, over legality and illegality, over constitutionality and unconstitutionality. We knew that in the end what they were clashing over was us, what to do with the blacks, and whether or not to start treating us as human beings. I despised all of them."

—Eldridge Cleaver, *Soul on Ice*

Sophisticates of the 1950s may have recognized Washington as a slow-moving city of Southern attitudes. Since it was officially positioned above Deep Dixie, however, and was known sometimes to suffer snow, I imagined it to be fully accredited Yankee territory possessed only of the most enlightened views. And so, when I came to Washington in late 1954 as assistant to a Texas congressman, I assumed our nation's capital to be a showplace of racial equalities and opportunities.

True, the city had only recently integrated its public schools, restaurants, and theaters. But as Texas had not yet managed such forward steps, I did not consider that Washington may have been tardy or incomplete in its accomplishments. Much of my nation's history remaining unexplored country for me, I accepted unquestioningly the fiction that our Constitution performed exactly as advertised. Though made cynical and wise in the ways of local or state politics, I rejected the notion that Congress could be anything other than a delegation of nature's noblemen rapidly forging a more perfect Union.

On that October morning when I arrived at Union Station after three days and two nights in a day coach, weary but inspired by my first glimpse of the Capitol's dome sunning in the morning's light, I reacted just as young Jimmy Stewart had in *Mr. Smith Goes to Washington:* my first order of business was to tour those fabled landmarks so familiar from photographs and old newsreels. By dark I had paid respects to Mr. Lincoln in his impressive memorial, had witnessed the honor guard changed at the Tomb of the Unknown Soldier, had gawked at the foot of Washington's Monument and from the steps of Jefferson's Memorial. I paid particular court to that ultimate Mecca most likely to excite even the lowliest second-banana American politician—the White House. One blushes at the

99

memory of how doggedly one attempted to locate the exact spot that would re-create an old photo branded in the memory, a photo of an ailing FDR taking the oath for a fourth Presidential term from a White House portico while a young soldier on crutches graced the foreground of a sparse wartime crowd. When I tried to explain to my puzzled tour guide my reasons for seeking multiple views of the White House, we experienced a total breakdown in communications.

For days I wandered Capitol Hill in a dizzy glow, rubbernecking for glimpses of famous faces. Whatever remains in me of the young country innocent still feels some small surge of electricity in remembering an early chance meeting in a Capitol corridor with—yes!—Vice-President Nixon! Though I had long judged Mr. Nixon a committed member of the ideological opposition, I extended the amnesty of a smile; he returned it and passed on by, leaving me disappointed only in that it did not seem proper for a common citizen to be so much taller than his Vice-President.

Whatever presumptive illusions I held about my capital city began to be dispelled in my search for family housing. Answering a classified ad boasting of numerous vacancies in a Southeast housing development, I was told that no vacancy existed. But the newspaper said— Sorry, the lady on the telephone insisted, but the ad had been in error. The next day, however, that advertisement again appeared. Doggedly, I again telephoned. Stubbornly, the voice affirmed that no vacancy existed. I reported my puzzling experience to an old Capitol Hill veteran, who smiled. "Go out there and apply in person," he said. "Landlords are getting pretty cautious about taking their tenants sight unseen." Though not grasping the full impact of his message, I complied. Five minutes after walking into the rental office I had my choice of apartments bordering on a wooded park and situated near a high hill overlooking the Capitol Building and all of downtown Washington. When I related my puzzling telephone experiences, the rental manager leaned across the counter and lowered his voice. "Well, you see, you've got a right obvious Southern accent. And well, no offense, for I come from North Carolina myself, but maybe our girl thought you might be one of the Colored." Then why in hell didn't his newspaper ad instruct potential tenants they must apply in person? "You draw too much attention to yourself that way," the man said. "It makes you too easy a target for troublemakers. The goddamn Colored are taking over this city."

The Negro was not taking over Capitol Hill, however. It soon became apparent that he was only a small part of democracy's daily operations. Some few atypical senators or congressmen had a showcase black or two on their staffs; one rarely saw the Negro among the several thousand Hill employees, however, except in his role as waiter, mailman, elevator operator, custodian, truck driver, or lower-echelon committee clerk. With a few exceptions, only Negro congressmen such as Adam Clayton Powell or Chicago's William Dawson trusted their black employees with anything more than minor tasks. When Congressman Powell arrived as a freshman in 1944, he was himself refused a haircut in the House of Representatives barber shop until he marched in rage to the Speaker.

The District of Columbia in 1954 was well on its way to becoming our first major city with a black majority, as Negroes coming to their Northern migrations from Virginia, the Carolinas, or other Dixie stations stopped and stayed on. Yet the District was ruled by congressional committees heavily weighted with powerful old Dixiecrats to whom "integration" had become the foulest word in the language. Their contributions to District schools ended with harassing a superintendent whom they blamed for excess enthusiasm in trying to make integrated classrooms work. Laws enacted by Congress permitted loan sharks, wig sellers, used-car tycoons, or other dollar-oriented types to prey on the black poor virtually without regulation. While adequate public housing was never raised, bus fares often were. Slums were knocked down not to provide decent low-cost housing but to reclaim preferred lands where private developers were thriving through their expensive high-rises and

chic town houses; displaced blacks were forced into other crowded ghettos. While officially Congress refused home rule to Washington because "Our forefathers intended this to be a federal city," one heard more than one statesman privately express his real fear: the election of a "nigger mayor" whom it would not do to have greeting Queen Elizabeth or Khrushchev, should they visit. A liaison man to Capitol Hill from the metropolitan police department understood why funds for the Police Boys Clubs were increasingly difficult to raise: nobody wanted to donate to "a bunch of little pickaninnies." A six-man congressional subcommittee chaired by old "Judge" James C. Davis of Georgia, and containing four Southern members, conducted an "investigation" originated by Mississippi's Representative John Bell Williams and "discovered"—to nobody's surprise—that Negroes were intellectually inferior.

The Texas State Society, comprised of several hundred Texans in Washington including Senate Majority Leader Lyndon B. Johnson and Speaker Sam Rayburn, then maintained segregation by requiring that multiple members in good standing sponsor all proposed new members; a select panel screened applicants. When word got around in 1955 that several young Turks might sponsor a black candidate, we received suggestions from congressional offices, well-connected lobbyists, old biddies known for their social pretensions, and others in the hierarchy that we ran the risk of embarrassing our bosses should we persist. (Old habits die hard. Almost a decade later, after a small number of blacks had been admitted to the Texas State Society following much internal turmoil, the organization began to choose through a select committee its annual Cherry Blossom Princess where she traditionally had been chosen by lottery from among the several candidates; significantly, this new control came into being only after a young black woman was rumored as a potential Princess. Precious ironies resulted: two Texas congressmen, each a power in his legislative specialty, gave near-fanatical backing to their respective daughters. Congressmen, lobbyists, military officers, social butterflies, and insignificant Hill clerks serving on the selection committee were subjected to such cruel pressures from competing Capitol Hill cartels that old friendships were broken, careers were blighted, and the wife of one senatorial aide retired in weeping fits to the sanctuary of a nervous breakdown.)

Perhaps one should not have expected natural democratic reflexes from so undemocratic an institution as the United States Congress, where one belongs to a certain caste as surely as if born in India. The powerful are jealous in the extreme of their prerogatives. Old birds who rise to chair influential committees by waiting out the slow seniority system are resentful of new men or fresh ideas; some actually snort in anger should a junior congressman innocently sit uninvited in a special nook of the House cafeteria, or they snub freshmen senators for exercising their rights of free speech when older and presumably wiser heads desire the floor. The more one considers how many bright young congressmen he saw become chair-warming drones in due erosion of time, the more one is amazed that any legislation tainted by the slightest scent of progress is ever passed.

Even in its internal operations, I learned, Congress rejected the notion of a society in which equality might thrive. Not only committee assignments but such mundane considerations as office suites, parking places, and the pecking order among congressmen relaxing over after-hours highballs depended on the virtues of seniority. I once witnessed a comic-opera scene in the House barber shop, where a junior congressman was thrice within a hair of being next, only to be displaced in his turn by the arrival of yet another powerful senior. Staff members coveted their own high stations within the hierarchy of Capitol Hill employees: the lordly administrative assistant to a congressional power was more revered than his colleague working for a junior member, and executive secretaries looked down their noses at common clerks.

Any congressman who arrived in Washington feeling a secret superiority to the Republic's commoners soon learned that nothing on Capitol Hill discouraged that particular vanity.

Well-heeled lobbyists, ambitious hostesses, famous generals or admirals, Cabinet members, nationally syndicated columnists, and occasionally even the President himself entertained him with fine foods, good wines, and shameless flattery. When he returned home between congressional sessions, the legislator found himself surrounded by his district's financial or political elite, men who welcomed him to their private clubs or to unusual opportunities for sound business investments, men who made the wheels go around, the cash registers jingle, or public opinion crystallize. In such heady circumstances it was easy for a congressman to forget that somewhere Americans were hungry, angry, without opportunity, deprived of their guaranteed rights—and that "somewhere" might be right over there across the railroad tracks or beyond some more invisible barrier in the congressman's own home town.

One hot day in 1955 Mrs. Rosa Parks, a black woman, had the temerity not to move to the back of an Alabama bus simply because her feet hurt and she was in no mood for games. When Montgomery authorities arrested her, a relatively unknown young minister named Martin Luther King, Jr., organized a bus boycott. Though the event made national headlines and occupied our television screens, I am afraid we on Capitol Hill were only marginally impressed. "Damn fool niggers," the friendly assistant to a Midwestern congressman said over our ritual morning coffee. "Let 'em walk if they want to. The silly bastards aren't gonna put corns on anybody's feet but their own."

I saw no reason to disagree with my friend's basic conclusion. As a student of politics I had often seen men of power crushingly impose their will on the have-nots. Far from recognizing the Montgomery bus boycott as the opening salvo in a racial revolution that is still very much with us, I assumed that Montgomery's blacks would eventually sneak back aboard the bus and quietly move to their rear stations.

Tempers did not improve in 1955 when Emmett Till, a fourteen-year-old black boy visiting from Chicago, was brutally killed for having whistled at a white woman in Mississippi.

This inspired angry speeches in Congress and outraged editorials in the press—but little else. The doctrine of "massive resistance" to the Supreme Court's school-desegregation decision was then taking firm root in the South. White Citizens Councils flourished, more respectable than the Ku Klux Klan, because they attracted those men who lived in the big white houses on the hill or the white-collar class rather than the unlettered lintheads from the textile plants or the mechanics who grew dirt under their fingernails.

In 1956, the schools in little Clinton, Tennessee, were ordered integrated by court decree. John Kasper, an erratic young zealot who became a moving spirit of the White Citizens Councils, agitated local emotions to the extent that the National Guard was called in. One night after the Clinton school had been bombed, I returned to my Washington apartment to find my five-year-old daughter, Cheryl, observing the television news in horror. "Daddy, why did somebody bomb that school?" I had never said much to my daughter about racial matters, other than to affirm generally that all men were created equal and to brand as unacceptable the use of derogatory racist terms. Now, I found myself unprepared to deal with her basic question. Well, I said, bad men who didn't want Negro children to go to school there had bombed it. "But *why?*" Well, some people mistakenly thought that whites were better than blacks. "That don't give them the right to bomb a school!" my daughter exclaimed. "They might kill a little child!" Yes, it was horrible; it was wrong. "It's crazy!" she said. "They should put those ole mean people in jail." Yes, they should. I hoped they would. My daughter was restive in her bed that evening; her demands for water and bathroom privileges, and uses of other sleep-stalling ruses, persisted long beyond the norm. Threatened with the rod, she tearfully identified the dark she feared at the top of her stairs: "Daddy, two Negro boys and two Negro girls go to my kindergarten class. I'm afraid the ole mean people will bomb it." I gave my personal word that such a tragedy would not happen, then sat on the edge of her bed trying to explain intelligently and soothingly an insane situation. It was not always easy to field her simple and direct little-girl questions: "But why doesn't President Eisenhower put a stop to it? He's the boss of the country!"

In my native Texas, Governor Shivers was then repelling school-desegregation orders in Texarkana and Mansfield; President Eisenhower, as earlier noted, made no moves to "put a stop to it." The doctrine of "interposition" (an obsolete notion that an individual state might impose its authority between the federal government and the state's citizens or institutions when convenient) was reviving throughout the South. Its larger champions in my home state included Governor Shivers, Attorney General John Ben Shepperd (who knew his own gubernatorial ambitions), and J. Evetts Haley, a right-wing rancher-writer himself seeking the governorship on a "Texans for America" platform. Early in his campaign, candidate Haley dispensed the following wisdom on a state-wide radio hookup:

> *"If you believe in the right of contract, and everyone but a Communist does, then you believe in interposition. If you look over a menu and order ham and eggs for breakfast, you have made a contract. If Brussels sprouts and beans are brought to you instead, you, as a partner in that contract, interpose your objections, and refuse to eat and pay for them. Interposition, in spite of all the political mumbo-jumbo, is just as Constitutional as ham and eggs."*

The Texas Legislature, in its unsubtle objective to put the NAACP out of business, passed a law requiring the organization to surrender its membership lists, financial records, or other papers to any judge so demanding. Attorney General Shepperd immediately discovered friendly judges throughout the state who willingly complied with this harsh new law; Texas Rangers swooped in to raid every NAACP chapter in the state. Shepperd shortly filed charges against the organization for evasion of state taxes, for making a profit while claiming nonprofit status, and vaguely for "engaging in unlawful political activity." Though a state court eventually reduced the charges and allowed the NAACP to function again, the attorney general's "crusade" effectively stymied the organization for almost a year.

Texas newspapers reacted to our home-grown McCarthys with cheers and accolades, making it no easier for more reasoning public officials to find courage in their souls. Nor did it help those of us in Congress when State Representative Joe Pool of Dallas (a portly mattress manufacturer who later as a congressman would sponsor a bill labeling as treason any utterance against the Vietnam War) came to Washington bearing his own version of the Southern Manifesto pledging, in effect, segregation forever. Pool circulated his petition among Texas congressmen while hinting that the press would soon know who had or had not Stood Up for Texas. Thanks to Senator Lyndon Johnson, just beginning seriously to imagine himself as President if luck should smile, counter-pressures were applied, so that less than half the twenty-three Texas congressmen signed. My own boss, who agonized in the matter, might very well have signed had not LBJ strong-armed him in the cause of decency. (The rumor was then going around that Brooks Hays, a moderate congressman from Arkansas, stared defeat in the face for his role in attempting to act as a peacemaker between President Eisenhower and Governor Faubus in the confrontation between state and federal authority attending integration of Little Rock's Central High. Such news made all Southern moderates nervous. When Congressman Hays ultimately was defeated by a staunch segregationist candidate in a write-in campaign, many so-called Southern moderates, discovering that evil was more easily performed than good, rushed to join their more rabid Dixie colleagues in segregationist proclamations or actions.)

Our west Texas congressional district was further inflamed by the 1957 civil-rights bill, mail running a hundred to one (or maybe a thousand to nothing) against. Not all the frightening sentiments came from sourdough cowboys or oilfield roughnecks: bankers' wives, newspaper reporters, ministers, oil-company bigwigs, old school chums, and Chamber of Commerce pitchmen wrote of Communist influences at large in Washington; I discovered that some few old Ivy League grads or New York natives who had migrated to Texas had easily adopted segregationist attitudes. The mayor of a thriving city told my congressman, "I feel like posting machine-gunners on the outskirts of town, and mowing down every federal son-of-a-bitch who comes down Highway 80." A bank president voiced his disillusion: "You young men want to change the rules. If I could find somebody seventy-five years old running for Congress, I'd vote for him without asking if he was Prohibitionist or Vegetarian. I'd figure him to have his racial pride."

I was host in Washington to a couple visiting from our grass-roots precincts—white, middle-class, powers in their little town; people to be shown a certain deference because of their special influences on their local newspaper and within the Democratic Party. One summer afternoon while driving around Potomac Park we saw parked at the river's edge a black man and a white woman taking the sun in a convertible; they were laughing and obviously enjoying each other. *"My God!"* the visiting Texas lady shouted. *"Did you see that?"* She turned and twisted for as far as the natural eye could follow, all the while proclaiming how such a sight made her sick to the core. My visitor next grew shrill over seeing several black men speed by in a large and well-chromed sedan: "That makes me so damned mad! Why do niggers drive such big ole cars? All they do is drive like crazy people and clutter up the highways!"

Yes, I said, it was a damned shame: they ought to make all the niggers stay home until white folks had reached their own destinations; my congressman would be happy to sponsor such a bill. Its particulars would require white people to call a central number when they had safely reached their homes or other targets. Only after all whites were accounted for could niggers take to their machines.

My guest had the grace to laugh as the barb struck, though she did insist, "Well, why *do* they all drive such big cars?" In the first place, I said, her sweeping generality did not hold: not *all* of them did, or anything like it. And perhaps those who did felt compelled to drive big cars because they had little enough going for them in other ways. I did not then have the benefit of the fuller explanation Julius Lester would offer in his writings: "In the black community, a Cadillac is a symbol of resistance, because its proud owner is refusing to be what the society wants him to be. His Cadillac is a weapon in his fight to tell himself that he is as much of a man as any white man."

My own congressman, harassed by his nay-saying constituents, and by nature something less than a raving integrationist, would not have voted for the 1957 civil-rights bill had not Senator Lyndon Johnson and Speaker Sam Rayburn—their efforts corresponding to LBJ's growing Presidential itch—kept the pressure on. Rayburn, still tough when it mattered to him, called the recalcitrant Texans in one by one: *Look here, Lyndon has a chance to be President. As President he can do you, your district, and your state a heap of good—or, if he wanted to, he could cause you right smart harm. But Lyndon don't have a snowball's chance in hell if you Texas boys vote against this bill. Adlai Stevenson and Jack Kennedy and the* New York Times *and that crowd will beat him to death with your votes and write him off as the candidate of Southern bigots. Lyndon's counting on you. And I'm counting on you.*

My man agonized to the last, despite a lecture from Rayburn at the Speaker's podium during the early moments of the roll call, and, having finally cast his vote for decency, turned his back to the press gallery, twisted his arm high behind his back as if a captive, and then grinned wryly to make clear the circumstance of his vote.

If my congressman's racial attitudes were less than wildly progressive, still he compared favorably with some. "As far as I'm concerned," said a Mississippi congressional assistant who later would be elected to the House, "a liberal is somebody who don't favor lynching on Sunday." A Texas congressman known for his vast store of funny stories was not at all amusing the evening I heard him explain why he no longer permitted the

Ed Sullivan Show to be piped into his home: "It's nothing but a black-pussy show. You can't turn it on without Eartha Kitt, Lena Horne, or some other black bitch twitching her butt all over your living room." One is discouraged even from attempting a complete list of the many times on Capitol Hill when one heard such emotions expressed, often triggered for reasons that one could not clearly discern. Even congressmen known to the public for their pro-civil-rights postures shocked now and again with their sly racist references or appreciations of "nigger jokes" in private moments.*

There were moments of unconscious dark humor. One occurred when Robert Weaver, a black man being questioned by a senatorial committee investigating his qualifications for appointment as administrator of the Federal Housing and Home Finance Agency, came face to face with an anachronistic interim senator from Texas, one William ("Dollar Bill") Blakely. Mr. Blakely, at least as rich as he was smart, was fond of posing for publicity pictures on horseback while dressed in the garb of the open range—fuzzing his image a bit, perhaps, by wearing French cuffs and diamond studs with his garish cowboy boots and Tom Mix hats. The official transcript of the Weaver hearings will verify the following exchange:

Senator Blakely : "I understand the August 1948 issue of *Masses and Mainstream,* the successor to *New Masses,* a Communist magazine, appears to review your book, *The Negro Ghetto. . . .*

Mr. Weaver: "Do you know who wrote it? I might be able to identify it better."

Senator Blakely: "Yes. This seems to be by J. Crow, realtor?"

Mr. Weaver: "Who?"

Senator Blakely: "J. Crow, realtor. Do you know J. Crow?"

Mr. Weaver: "I did not know he wrote book reviews."

Laughter.

---

* Many Southern legislators, when knowingly writing to black constituents, began "Dear Friend" so as to avoid calling them "Mr." or "Mrs." The envelopes carrying such friendly letters were addressed only to "Willie Jones" or "Bessie Walker."

There was limited social mingling among the races in Washington in the late 1950s and early 1960s. Mild friendships existed with blacks among those few Hill employees who had risen above the broom or delivery carts, with others who came from executive-agency middle ranks, a smattering of newsmen, lawyers, doctors, military officers, or embassy attachés.

These were from among the Negro elite; few of them discussed race except with obvious reluctance. They had struggled out of their own private ghettos or up from early disappointments, and now they wanted to forget; one soon discovered that not only the night watchman's son desired social assimilation more than was good for his character. (One of the most beautiful women I have known, a Hill secretary who claimed to be Filipino, was discovered to be the daughter of an unmistakably Negro woman when I paid an unexpected social call to her apartment one evening.) These blacks who had gained at least marginal assimilation might have served as bridges of understanding to a small but influential segment of the white world.

Possibly I do them a disservice: perhaps many had experienced so many rejections, had seen the white man trot out his obvious and his more subtle prejudices so often, that they had simply despaired. "A white man ought to assume that if the Negro before him is twenty-five years old, he has had twenty, if not twenty-five, years of insults and rebuffs, and that that Negro may have had quite enough," John A. Williams has written. "A white man ought to assume that, and if he had any sense he would."

Those black men or women with whom I shared passing associations were better instinctive judges of my racial understandings or commitments than I. For, though I assumed myself enlightened to a fault and unusually "democratic," mine was a mild liberalism more comfortable than not in its executions. Lip service to the cause of racial justice I generously paid, never hesitating to deplore the latest bombing in Birmingham; priding myself on giving George Lincoln Rockwell the bum's rush when he crossed the Potomac from his American Nazi

Headquarters in Arlington to distribute racist pamphlets in the halls of Congress; berating my Hill colleagues because they looked without seeing the miserable slums existing in Washington; righteously snubbing Governor Orval Faubus at a Jefferson–Jackson Day dinner in the Mayflower Hotel; cheering from long distance those young North Carolina blacks who first suffered white spittle, arrests, and brutal beatings in attempting to integrate lunch counters; and proclaiming my approval of the Warren Court.

Yet, what were my special accomplishments? I saw the black ghettos against which I raged only in driving my weekly cleaning woman to her hovel in the slums, or in attending sports events in old Griffith Stadium. (And though I fretted over the obvious squalor and hopelessness in those dark Washington slums, I was perhaps equally concerned that blacks made hostile by my Texas car tags might slash my tires as I witnessed the baseball Senators or the football Redskins at the malpractice of their chosen professions.) We well-fed white liberals who sat in our suburban homes congratulating ourselves and mankind on the passage of tame civil rights bills, or cheering edicts by the Warren Court, were pathetically tardy in understanding that such actions were of small moment in the absence of enthusiastic enforcement at all levels of government. We were too easily pleased by official statistics showing high numbers of blacks to be employed or in integrated schools, not pausing to consider that figures could conceal as well as reveal: how many blacks earned sums equal to their white counterparts even in the same jobs? How many were office managers as opposed to porters? How many white children were being whisked by their alarmed parents away from integrated schools so that de facto segregation soon would reign? What was gained by desegregating lunch counters or theaters if the black citizen could not afford the price of sandwiches or tickets? Though I worked with some few men of decent instincts in Texas on behalf of what we considered progressive legislation helpful in solving "the Negro problem," I did so surreptitiously, like a thief in the night, so as not to arouse the more honest bigots. When the Freedom Rides began rolling South and I was moved to join them, neither my Congressman nor my former wife had difficulty persuading me against that course, by citing dangers to my political sponsor, to my family, or to my physical person. And though I urged full integration of the public schools, my own children attended those schools in the District of Columbia where, because of financial considerations or due to restrictive covenants in real-estate contracts, only a smattering of black children might be found.

Even one who softly proclaimed his belief in racial justice or who still shamefully harbored some persistent old half-conscious racial prejudice, however, was likely to be harshly judged by hard-core segregationists back home. On trips back to Texas during congressional adjournments or recesses I found old friends as difficult in their attitudes as were more faceless members of our constituency.

Worth was a radio announcer, an old high-school classmate once known for his excellent grades and pious aspirations to the ministry; together we had enjoyed many youthful pursuits. By the late 1950s, however, Worth had become so outspokenly racist as to make rational conversation impossible: his smallest observations were replete with gratuitous references to nigger lips, noses, brains, hair, feet, sex equipment, or shiftless habits.

One evening in the early 1960s Worth gave a dinner party to which I was attracted for professional reasons: he controlled the flow and content of local news for his radio station, and I was a paid flack shilling the re-election of my congressman. Other guests included Elder, an oil-company white-collar worker whom I had also known since high school; Jack, the owner of the radio station where Worth was employed; Cole, a representative of a local advertising agency; and their respective wives. What came out as the evening wore on and drinks flowed is offered as representative of the drawing-room conversations of the period.

Elder opened with a salvo against the Supreme Court, attributing its decisions to instructions contained in the Communist Manifesto. Jack, the radio-station owner, who displayed an IMPEACH EARL WARREN bumper sticker on his car, attacked Congress for knuckling under to the Court's edicts. The advertising man warmly endorsed the long-gone doctrine of interposition. Worth proposed direct election of Supreme Court justices to fixed terms. The wives sang out their loyalties to states' rights and a rigid Constitution. Eventually my long silence drew attention. Worth rather belligerently solicited my agreement.

No, I did not agree. The Constitution was a living document, capable of growing or being expanded to meet new conditions; it had, in fact, been amended numerous times. Its framers had known, or sensed, that history did not stand still, and so had provided the machinery for orderly change. One Congress could not bind another to its past actions, as example, thereby clearing the way for lawful adjustments. The Supreme Court existed as a source of the people's final appeal, a safety-valve to insure against our lawmakers' robbing us of our basic freedoms in their rush to ratify the prevailing prejudices of their constituents. To protect the court from those day-to-day political pressures capable of swaying elective officials from their more reasoned judgments, our high court justices were appointed to lifetime terms unless they chose to resign or could be removed for crimes of moral turpitude or high treason. Nor did I agree that states' rights could be properly invoked ahead of those human rights promised each American in the Bill of Rights. The Constitution had made clear, and our higher courts had affirmed, that our nation had been established not as a loose collection of sovereign states each a law unto itself, but as satellites of a larger, central, *united* union.

My little elementary civics lecture was not permitted to be delivered in one smooth flow, however. There were general grumblings, one or two challenges to specific points, impatient shufflings.

"Bullshit," Elder said. "Sounds like the Commie line to me. You've been off up yonder in the East too long."

"Elder," I said, "it's the same damn thing we were taught in school, though probably more clearly stated."

"All I remember is about the Alamo and our forefathers standing up for their rights," he said.

"Well, what did they teach you at the university?"

"They damn sure didn't teach me nigger-loving," Elder said, flushing and glaring. He relaxed when Worth and the wives cheered, signifying his right to claim the point.

"Admit it," the radio magnate urged. "Don't you think they should impeach Earl Warren?"

"On what grounds?"

"All those communistic decisions. Hell, they've got *plenty* of grounds. All they need is guts."

"You can't impeach a justice for the opinions he returns! Hell, interpreting the law is his goddamn *job*, Jack!"

"But the Warren Court's decisions run to a pattern, don't you see? All these goddamn opinions forcing the races to mix and mingle . . . letting the labor unions run over everybody . . . taxing business people to the nines just to keep deadbeats on welfare! You said yourself that justices can be impeached for high treason. Now why isn't all *that* treason?"

"You badly misrepresent the Court's actions," I said. "You might profit by looking up the definition of treason."

"So you don't think there's grounds to impeach 'em?"

"No."

"*Why,* by God?"

"Shit, he can't tell you," Elder charged.

"I sure as hell can't," I flared, "because we're too far apart in our concepts. Let's talk about football, or sex."

The radio king smiled, vastly pleased. "I knew he'd backwater."

I was weary and more than willing to permit my banners to remain drooping in the dust: why agitate people whose broadcast facilities we might otherwise bend to our political advantage? What might be gained by shouting invectives through the long whiskey night, in an atmosphere where the first fumes of reason surely would evaporate the moment they were exposed to the wild and mindless air? I sat silent, brooding over my drink, yearning for the less personally dangerous bigotries of Washington, while there passed around the circle wholesale condemnations of Walter Reuther, "Martin Luther Coon," the goddamned Kennedys, Dwight D. Eisenhower (who had permitted Khrushchev to visit America, with those dangerous old Communist ideas in his head), Castro, Lyndon Johnson, the United Nations, *Time* magazine (one of the ladies was slightly confused in that she recalled Alger Hiss as having been a *Time* editor rather than Whittaker Chambers), the NAACP, Franklin, and Eleanor.

"FDR started all the trouble," Jack Radio said. "He encouraged the Nigras to congregate Up North when he put the country on a damned welfare binge."

"And that silly ole Eleanor," Worth's wife added. "You couldn't pick up a paper without she was kissing a nigger or holding dances for 'em in the White House."

I demurred: FDR had been more talk than action in the civil rights department. True, his federal work or relief programs to combat the Depression had assisted blacks as well as whites. Still, Negroes had remained underpaid and unemployed compared to their white brothers; they had remained segregated in their schools or slums; in the South they could not vote, had been shoved to the back of the bus, and had been repeatedly lynched or otherwise terrorized. Perhaps so many Negroes had gone North because of their maltreatment in the South, or to claim jobs during World War II.

Elder and Worth had begun to exchange their favorite nigger jokes even before my dissent was complete. Elder's belligerent posture was increasingly proportional to his intake of bourbon highballs; I could feel a small whiskey flush on my own cheeks.

"I tell you one thing," Elder said. "One of those burr-headed little apes touches my daughter in school, and I'll break his friggin' arms down to nubs." (Elder's daughter was then in the seventh grade in a school system in the process of racially integrating one grade each year, beginning with the first grade. Obviously, she would be graduated before black hands might soil her. More rage than arithmetic was in Elder's head, however.)

"There's three nigger kids in my little Billy's room," a mother proclaimed. "I told him not to play with 'em. I told him be *nice* . . . just don't *play* with 'em."

"I catch my kids playing with 'em," Elder said, "and I'll bust their butts. Niggers don't have the sense God gave a bore monkey. They was off somewhere drinking gin when brains was passed around."

I had fully intended to keep my silence, and probably would have, had the room not jumped with mirth at Elder's latest witticism.

"Goddamn you, Elder," I said. "I've known black people smarter than both of us."

Elder blew out of his chair, enraged, sloshing whiskey over a wide perimeter. "They may be smarter than *you*, you sonnuvabitch, but you don't know any goddamn niggers smarter than *I* am." He flailed his long pale skinny arms and screeched profanities, an altogether wild bird, and for the first time I realized just how easy it might be to call up a lynch mob from among my old friends.

In the quick thick silence following Elder's outburst I turned to the host. "Worth, it's go or have a goddamn fistfight. I think I'll just go."

"Then go *on*," Worth's wife said. "I don't see you tied to anything."

"Go on back up there with the rest of the Communists," Elder shouted, and I stumbled out thinking *I don't believe it this can't be happening I've known these guys twenty years.*

Worth and Jack followed me to my car. Worth, though tipsy, was tense and ill-at-ease, torn between loyalties to an old friend whose ideas he now judged spoiled and those beliefs he shared with Elder and the others, beliefs that made him dizzy with outrage at what the niggers and Reds and pie-eating politicians were doing to his country. "I sure hate this happening," he said, "but maybe you brought it on yourself." Well, maybe, I said, but let's just forget it. "You really *have* been off up there too long," Worth said. "You've been brainwashed by 'em." My anger came back new and full: "Worth, you ass, when was the last time you read a book? I mean that! What was the last goddamn book you read?" Worth was honestly startled: "Not since college, I guess. But I listen to radio and television. I know what's going on in the world."

Jack attempted to be conciliatory. He took my arm as I started to climb into the car. "Now understand," he said, "while I don't agree with you, I'm not a nut on the subject like Elder is—ole Elder, he loses his head sometimes. I don't think *all* Nigras are bad, or that everybody in Washington's a Communist. But I don't think even half of 'em want this integration."

"Jack, please don't tell me how your maid or your gardner told you that. I heard the same story at the Country Club last night from three different sources—all of 'em eating ten-dollar steaks."

"Well, they don't! It's the cheap politicians stirring everything up! Hell, I don't see anybody mistreating Nigras around here. You'd think we kept slaves to hear the Washington politicians! Maybe some Nigras don't have as much as they might— but hell, *I* got more money than ole Worth here's got. He works for *me*. That's the way things are! The goddamn Supreme Court can't make everybody the same. That's what Communism is! Some work and some won't, some do and some don't."

Elder had now materialized in the door, a long loose silhouette waving his cranelike arms and spouting midnight gibberish. The sight caused the realization that I was more than a toe juiced in my own right, perhaps dangerously so, perhaps only a word away from inspiring my old friends to a collective ass-kicking. So I climbed into the car and drove away, clucking conciliatory sounds.

For an hour or more I drove the dark streets of that little West Texas town, remembering schoolboy adventures shared with Worth and Elder: outings in our Boy Scout troop, trips to Fort Worth to witness the annual Fat Stock Show and Rodeo, juke-box dances at the Teen Center, midnight visits to the pussy salesmen working the Crawford Hotel. Once, in a showdown to see who could drink the most whiskey straight from a jug while riding the train to Fort Worth, I had passed out just beyond Big Spring while Elder had upchucked from about Abilene on. And once, during a summer Youth Crusade for Christ at the First Baptist Church, Worth—then with thoughts of becoming a minister—had come to me during the invitational hymn, speaking so persuasively of the joys of heaven that I had followed him down the aisle there to proclaim my personal salvation while the choir sang, the visiting evangelist shouted hosannas, and witnessing high-school halfbacks wept while promising themselves and Jesus never again to enjoy the pleasures of border-town Mexico.

We had known so many common experiences, the same teachers and preachers and friends. We had parents whose attitudes were strikingly similar. We had served in the military in the same era. How, then, to account for our wildly divergent views on race, or in political matters? Why were we all so angry, so *certain,* from our opposite sides of the ideological or emotional fence? I had read more than Worth or Elder, had gone out to see more of the big world and had stayed longer. Could it be that simple? But that only led back to the root question of *why* I had been influenced to read or inquire where Elder or Worth had not; *why* I had sought out the world while they had stayed home to build barricades against it. If man was as strongly influenced by his environment in the formative years as I had come to believe through reading novels and touches of sociology, and through my personal observations, then how to account for the great differences in men's hearts and heads when they considered the most basic of human rights or the most elemental of social questions? I did not puzzle out the answer before dropping off to sleep at dawn in my motel bed.

Worth and Elder represented the crudest sort of racism, but

they were not alone. Even in genteel surroundings where tasteful oil paintings hung from the walls or men took their brandy with cigars without talking of football or "niggers," there occurred unexpected embarrassments. One evening, as the guest of an oil man who had founded his own company and built a huge stone mansion I privately thought of as grander than one of Mussolini's better railroad stations, I sat with a frozen smile while the well-oiled oil king urged his Negro bartenders and caterers to entertain with tap dances and songs. "Come on now," he coaxed. "I got five dollars for the first song and dance. Hell, *ten* dollars." "Sir," one of the black men protested, "we just don't sing and dance." "*All* you boys sing and dance," the oil baron insisted. Nervous glances were exchanged among the dozen well-dressed guests and there was a swapping of taut smiles; the more sensitive dipped their heads down in deep contemplation of their shoes. Our host was a big man, a power who might profitably encourage the ambitious or assist the favored in their goals, and so even the most offended among us smiled frozen smiles—and said nothing.

Sometimes one was strangely touched by men who expressed their fears and prejudices in soft terms; one recognized them as bigots, for sure, but one's own polarization against prevailing white attitudes was not yet complete. And so something in the blood stirred in slow, sad sympathy at the most unexpected moments. "I know it's wrong," an old barber blurted one afternoon after stopping me on the streets of Midland to register his complaints against pending civil rights legislation. "I can look around and see we ain't treated colored people exactly right. I *know* that. And I guess change is gonna come. But I'm old and set in my ways and I can't seem to favor it." And there was an old judge, a flinty character famed for throwing the book at offenders against the law, who surprisingly volunteered over coffee in a little West Texas cafe, "I live in fear that some Negro is gonna file a lawsuit to integrate our school or test whether he can sit at that table over there and eat a hamburger—and I'll have to rule on it. There's no doubt in my mind a Negro has a right to go to any tax-supported school you can find, and in my heart I think he has the right to eat wherever he can afford to pay his check. But I just flat can't say if I've got enough guts to rule that way. I wouldn't mind being defeated for reelection so much, if it came to that—hell, they wouldn't be getting any cherry. It's all the old friends I'd lose . . . the abuse I'd be forced to take from people I've known since I was a pup. And I'm not confident I'd be strong enough to survive that."

One grew to prefer confrontations with flaming bigots more confident in their prejudices. It was not difficult for my congressman to order to hell white extremists mobilized to prevent blacks from moving into a formerly segregated section of Midland: they had harmed their cause by leading a mob throwing stones and bricks and chanting hate. One could, therefore, even show a small political profit in damning them. We knew that our district, while certainly strong in segregationist sentiments and practices, fancied itself enough advanced over Mississippi (or even deep East Texas) to be repelled by Ku Kluxer tactics. Our businessmen knew that maximum profits could never be realized in communities torn by racial violence, and many of our transplants from New England or Scarsdale were civilized enough to reject what they thought of as hillbilly conduct. Even Junior Leaguers who told you over pre-dinner martinis how their black maids tended to have sticky fingers, even the distressed barber or the flinty old judge, would not endorse violence in those pre-white-backlash days. So we were free to hoot and dance our occasional public defiance against the well-discredited. And managed, somehow, to feel almost righteous about it.

There was as yet no compelling reason to clamor for "law and order" as the white society now defines it, for the black man had not yet begun to shoot back. It was too bad, in the old days of the early 1960s, when grinning cops stood by while enraged whites rubbed mustard or ketchup in the hair of well-dressed, carefully barbered black students attempting to integrate Southern lunch counters—and, having wearied of that sport, beat and kicked them. Tsk! Tsk! Tsk! And shamey-shame! The concerned bravely flayed old Bull Connor's slashing police dogs and pressurized fire hoses capable of felling a man as effectively as a club. We cried shame at the campus tormentors of Autherine Lucey and Charlayne Hunter . . . knocked the mob at Ole Miss so anxious to rip James Meredith apart that it fought all night against armed federal marshals . . . made speeches against those fiends who had bombed to death little black girls in starched dresses in their Birmingham Sunday-school class. We condemned the burning of the Freedom Ride buses, the murders in Mississippi of student civil rights workers, the beatings at Selma Bridge, the packed jails in dozens of Southern hamlets where blacks following the nonviolent preachments of Martin Luther King sang songs of freedom or prayed while their racist jailers thought up new tortures or humiliations. You name it, we deplored it, and said somebody should do something about it. And nobody much did. Including us.

When we attempted to do the humane or "right" thing it was more often than not a meaningless gesture, or some unthinking act the long-range consequences of which we need not face. I am reminded of one of my own thoughtless acts, occurring as I drove my family toward Texas upon the adjournment of Congress in the early 1960s.

We were in the area of Mississippi where Charles Mack Parker (another young black alleged to have wanted his way with a white woman) had been dragged from jail by a mob and horribly killed. We had decided against stopping for lunch at a restaurant—partly because we wanted to roll on down the highway, partly because I had always found that section of Mississippi so brooding and sullen that I felt uncomfortable breathing its air. When we came to an isolated general store near the road's edge, I stopped to buy cold drinks and sandwich makings.

I arrived behind a half-dozen or more blacks, rural people in wretched old clothes, the kids barefoot, all with the dust of an adjacent field on them. Though the one adult black man in the group had already admitted his companions to the store before spotting me, he obsequiously stepped away from the door at my approach, snatched his old felt hat from his head, and, mumbling Uncle Tomisms through his ghastly parody of a smile, made clear by elaborate gestures that I should precede him. We performed an Alphonse-Gaston act which I finally lost, he having more experience at patiently waiting.

The black man's wife and several stair-step children were at the meat counter, pointing out their preferences: bologna, cheese, frankfurters. Quite without thinking about it, and while waiting my turn, I inspected the general store's rolls of chicken wire, stacks of Boss Walloper work gloves, tins of snuff, Moon Pies, and R.C. Colas, broad-brimmed straw hats, and other staple treasures indigenous to the rural stores of my Texas youth. Lost in nostalgia, I did not respond to the owner, a thirtyish fat white man in a soiled apron, until he had several times addressed me.

"I said what can I do fer you?" he repeated for maybe the fourth or fifth time.

"These folks are ahead of me," I said.

"They can wait," he snapped.

"No, thanks. They were here first."

Only then did I realize the depth of the storekeeper's anger. Now began a nervous flickering of eyes among the blacks. I do not recall that they visibly moved, though there was some sense of restless motion, of uneasy winds blowing in a wheat field just before a sudden rainstorm, of deer standing with their noses in the air and trembling almost imperceptibly the instant before they fled some deadly danger.

"Tell me what you *wont!*" the storekeeper demanded.

Now I was mad. "Serve these people first."

The black man came forward from his station to my rear, hat in hand, shuffling and bowing, making tight little gestures indicating that I should claim my white right. I was on the verge of refusing, of foolishly forcing the issue wherever it might go, for the adrenaline was rising and the blood of some unrecorded old mean Irish-Scotch-German ancestor cried out for new holy wars. Then I saw the pleading in the black man's eyes, felt the breathless tensions of his brood, and tardily understood: soon I would be gone, zipping down the highway in my air-conditioned car at careless speeds, while these miserable human cattle would remain behind to suffer the dangerous fruits of the white man's foul humor.

The storekeeper prepared my order without comment, slamming food and drink bottles on the counter, speaking only in numbers to state the total cost. I was keenly aware of how cautiously alert the black customers remained, even unto the smallest child. I wanted somehow to make amends, to apologize, to communicate that I had intended them no trouble. But there was just no way, short of inciting the porky storekeeper to new rages or complications. Before I reached my car, I heard the rise of his angry backwoods whine.

For miles on down country, as the sun placed dazzling pool-like mirages on the flat Mississippi roadbed, I could imagine in them the reflection of that wretched rural black man, soiled old felt hat in hand, performing his obligatory dance of shame in the presence of his quietly outraged family.

I had an honest, easy rapport with only one black man in those congressional years. Moe and I were thick during the Kennedy era, when some racial progress—however reluctant—hovered in the air. He was then in his forties, working on Capitol Hill under the patronage of a California senator. Moe had originally come from the Denver slums, was a long-time Los Angeles resident and an Army veteran, and had pieced together three years of college by attending nights and in short stretches as his pocketbook permitted. Though he was a minor functionary in the United States Senate Post Office, Moe was hip to what was happening to a degree that continues to escape many of our public officials, educators, editors, or others of the opinion-making elite.

Moe warned four or five years before Watts that a Watts was destined to happen—though he predicted that ghetto outbursts would first occur in the great cities of the East, which he considered much more segregationist and cruel than the West Coast. Over many a drink and until numerous dawns he re-

viewed the rot and ruin of his black world, the white man's in-
difference, his own remembered humiliations.

"Driving across country," he said, "black people key their
kidneys to their gasoline tanks. We know there are more mean
bastards than not; we don't assume anything good. So we pull
up to the gas tanks when we get nature's urge, but before we
ask the man to fill 'er up we inquire if his rest room is open. If
we get turned down, we drive on to the next station." He told
how blacks pass the word among the traveling brothers: this is
"a good town," that one's "a shit town"; here you can safely
rent a motel room, there they might lynch you for trying. "Even
with all the tips you can pick up," he said, "you stay jumpy and
nervous. When you see a black man stagger into his motel after
a day on the road, he's weary for reasons other than the highway and the traffic. If you'll notice, black people drive within
the speed limits more than whites—because cops are quicker to
bust 'em. If a black man has car trouble it will be ten times
more difficult to get anybody to stop to help him, and when he
gets to a garage they'll stick him for all they can. And in any
emergency on the road, it's almost impossible for a black man
to get his check accepted without going to a local bank, un-
dergoing lengthy grilling, and then paying for long-distance telephone calls to his own bank, to his boss, or to anybody else
Mr. Charley chooses to touch base with. One time a bank in
Pennsylvania wouldn't take a check of mine until they'd cleared
me with the police. Wanted to be sure the FBI didn't have a
flyer out on me, I guess."

One evening when liquor had worked on Moe while we sat
in his small efficiency (from which he had a great view of the
spotlighted Capitol dome if not the darkened slums directly behind it), he said, "I'm not talking shit, and I'm not crying on
your ofay shoulder. For a black man, I've got it made. At least
I don't have a survival problem. I lay the truth on a few whites
I think capable of understanding and, more than that, caring—
otherwise, why bother? And I'm not telling it like it is because
I love the white man so goddamn much. Nobody much is telling Whitey what the black dude is feeling, or how full he is in

his craw. And Mr. Charley isn't straining anything to find out. The goddamn thing's gonna blow up in his face one day, and then he's gonna wonder how he got something nasty in his hair."

Sometimes Moe sounded militant, sometimes tame. When he heard, through the gossip of children, that one of my neighbors in a solidly white middle-class Washington residential section had complained of interracial parties in my home, he seemed more amused than angry or embarrassed. Yet, when I retaliated on the crotchety neighbor (by urging free beer on a four-man crew of ghetto blacks working with me in my yard one Saturday, to the point where their more uninhibited street expressions violated the surburban air), Moe was not only not amused, he was outraged. "You're not helping anybody by showboating," he complained. "You're just agitating tensions. Hell, *I* wouldn't want those 14th Street cats drunk, cussing, and cutting up in my neighborhood. You've made black people look bad by trying to get revenge on some miserable ofay prick not worth your trouble." "How'd you like to explain to your son why you couldn't buy him an ice-cream soda in a white drug-store on a hot day, or take him in a hotel lobby to piss when his little bladder's bursting?" he asked one night, coolly furious, when a white Hill secretary suggested that perhaps blacks were "pushing too fast." On the other hand, faced with that peculiar breed of white who thinks he must tell racist jokes to blacks by way of establishing his own easy sophistication, Moe sometimes laughed when I wondered how he could.

At a swimming party around his apartment pool, I heard Moe tease a comely young black schoolmarm visiting from South Carolina because she had not abandoned the South for less restrictive societies. South Carolina was her home, the young woman said in her defense, and, besides, things weren't always as dismal in Dixie as pictured. Most of the assembled blacks laughed or hooted.

Moe grinned. "Next thing, you'll be telling us you're close to Strom Thurmond."

"He talked to me once," the young woman said.

"Oh? And what did he say, Sister?"

"Well, I saw him at the railroad station. And I said, 'Hello, Senator Thurmond,' and he said—"

"And *he* said," Moe broke in, " 'Hello, *gurl!'*

The startled young woman looked at Moe as if perhaps he qualified as a soothsayer. *"Yeah!"* she said over the group laughter. "But how did *you* know?"

One night my friend knocked on my door at midnight. "I'm all packed," Moe said. "Going home to California." His sponsoring senator had failed to provide a promised better job, George Washington University had reneged on accepting credits to be transferred from USC, and he could no longer tolerate the depressing influences of the East. "This is shitbird country," he said over our final drinks. "Not much better than your dear ole Dixie. Sometimes I think the Confederacy won the fucking war."

He telephoned from Los Angeles the night of John F. Kennedy's assassination, and we cried together; I telephoned him some months later at five a.m. to discover him as inebriated, gloomy, and incoherent as I was. We have had no contact since.

Except as handy straw men for demagogues to flay, black people were not a political factor in our west Texas congressional district. Few lived there; a minority of these troubled to vote. When I placed a Negro school official on the list to receive my congressman's weekly newsletter (a distinction held by a mere twenty thousand people plus all possible newspaper, radio, and television outlets), he troubled to thank my congressman for "the nicest thing a politician ever did for me."

In the little cowtown of Marfa, where the townsfolk liked to brag that James Dean, Rock Hudson, and Elizabeth Taylor had come to shoot *Giant,* the film version of Edna Ferber's mild critique of Texas society, there lived but one black man. Lum was of indefinite years; for three decades he had been the shine "boy" and general handyman in the town's barber shop. One afternoon as we campaigned among cowboys, workingmen, and small shop keepers, Lum approached to inquire discreetly whether my congressman might be offended should he ask to shake his hand. He was embarrassingly joyous over being granted his small request, so much so that on our subsequent visits to Marfa we could expect Lum to be waiting at curbside in a necktie and an old black coat he obviously considered necessary to his greeting missions.

"I seen in the papers you was gonna be here today," Lum would say as he stuck out his hand. "Everybody in town's for you, if they tell the truth in my shop. No need for you to worry over Marfa."

"Ole Lum, he must of poked his head outta that barbershop nine dozen times today," some old rancher might chuckle.

And another would drawl, "Yeah, he was so eager we about figgered you'd made him campaign manager. But then somebody else said he heard that yawl had gone in partners in the chicken-stealing business." Titters and guffaws in the crowd.

"Lum, you got anything you want him to tell Kennedy for you?" another spectator might ask. There would be more smiles and laughter while the black man said seriously, No, he had just wanted to shake the congressman's hand. Then he would fade to the fringes of the crowd to listen silently while the villagers begged for higher farm subsidies, or a new post office, before cussing the Kennedys for their socialistic exercises.

Perhaps twice in eight years my congressman addressed black audiences; for one thing, he wasn't invited, and, for another, his time might simply be better spent. When our financial or ideological allies gathered in the home of this banker or that lawyer to plot campaign techniques or otherwise assist the congressman, no blacks appeared. At some larger function in a hotel ballroom or a restaurant's private dining room, when our field troops were rallied for exhortations against the latest campaign foe, one might find a rare black physician, black minister, or black school official sitting in the back row or standing self-consciously in a far corner. Not until 1961, when my congressman addressed an organization of Democratic women in

Midland, did we find seated before the roast beef and green peas a high percentage of blacks. "We *had* to take 'em into the organization," a local white leader confided. "Midland is such a Republican hotbed we didn't have enough warm bodies to stuff envelopes or nail up campaign posters." We always carried our black precincts by satisfying margins, however, for the opposition was generally so wrongheaded and reactionary that we looked better than our stains.

In 1962 (when a Republican troglodyte would defeat my conservative Democrat), worried and fearing democracy's verdict, I discovered while checking polling places in Odessa in midafternoon that blacks simply were not voting. I sought out the local black baron on whom we relied for whatever political influence we had among Negroes. "Sam," I said, "your people aren't voting. Let's get them to the polls."

"I been trying to get the cats out all day," Sam said. "They don't have much appetite for it."

I was angry: "Goddammit, have they forgotten the votes for civil rights bills? And votes for minimum-wage bills, public housing, a dozen other things that Republican bastard would die before he'd vote for?"

"Maybe they have," Sam said, looking out from the rickety two-chair barbershop across the waste and shanties of the local Flats. "Them things don't seem to have made much difference around here, now, do they, laddie?"

Perhaps "them things" didn't make much difference in Odessa, Watts, Newark, or Mississippi. There was a time when I believed they had: believed that the lunch-counter sit-ins had made a difference, the Freedom Rides through Dixie, the bus boycott in Montgomery, the march on Selma Bridge.

I believed it most strongly on a sun-dappled day in August 1963, when Dr. Martin Luther King had his dream in the shadow of the Lincoln Memorial. We thrilled to that dream and to the fantastically huge, orderly, singing, loving crowd of all shades and hues, backgrounds and heritages, opportunities and privations. America seemed ready to deliver its ancient promises: we had made laughingstocks of panicky congressmen who had predicted blood in Washington's streets, had closed their offices and sent their secretaries home to lock themselves in against gang rapes.

My friend Richard Gallagher, a writer with whom I attended the Freedom March activities, sent me a note on returning to New York:

> *Coming down on the charter train that fresh Freedom morning, it was a love feast. Brotherhood. Forgiveness. Unity. Let-my-people-go. Please, won't you take my seat and how about sharing my coffee cake, and, Brother, have you met my wife? Going back on the train that night, after King's big dream, everybody was their usual bitchy griping selfish suspicious selves, growling how you should get your fucking feet out of the goddamn aisle, and what mother-raper had stolen their sack lunch? I hope it ain't an omen.*

I might have been more skeptical of the long-range benefits of the Freedom March had I paused to consider that at its inception President Kennedy had been so fearful of its consequences that he made unavailing efforts behind the scene to cancel it. Only when that ploy failed and the Kennedy Administration felt an urgent need to make the Freedom March "respectable" enough to attract a broad base of support from whites and blacks affiliated with the less militant organizations was it officially endorsed. In retrospect, one sees this as the co-opting influence it proved. Bayard Rustin, who now cautions against black rage erupting into violence, and whose pitch for black capitalism is often difficult to distinguish from Richard Nixon's, was attacked by congressmen who opposed his leading role in the Freedom March as a sexual deviate, a former felon, and a probable Communist. Doctor King himself was then considered a dangerous figure by much of the white population, but was generally judged more palatable than Rustin or younger blacks on the rise. Thus the Kennedy Administration urged Doctor King to assume the leadership role of the Freedom March, pledging in return its cooperation and endorsement.

Administration sources also used their influence to tone down a militant speech full of hard truths by John Lewis of the Student Nonviolent Coordinating Committee. These behind-the-door activities were unknown to those of us who marched and sang on that happy day, however.

On November 22, 1963, I was lunching in the Democratic Club at the Congressional Hotel with a former congressman when a flurry of excitement at the bar caught our attention. "Turn it up!" somebody shouted. There on the television screen was the stricken face of Walter Cronkite telling us that President Kennedy's motorcade had been fired on in Dallas and that witnesses reported the President appeared to be bleeding from the head. Carl Albert of Oklahoma, then House Majority Leader, began to trot aimlessly around the room, pale and wild-eyed, darting this way and that, chaos and panic obviously sloshing in his mind, no plan or purpose yet possible. My luncheon companion repeated endlessly, "Oh my God, oh my God, oh my God. . . ." I looked two tables to my right, where Walter Jenkins, then the top administrative aide to Vice-President Lyndon Johnson, had been lunching with ex-Senator Earl Clement of Kentucky; they had disappeared. Carl Albert, his poor reeling brain recovering enough to let him run in a straight line, bolted from the room followed by other stunned congressmen, their administrative aides, or secretaries.

My companion and I sat staring at the television set; I remember that three or four black waiters stood in a tight knot near the bar, looking up at Cronkite, and one of them clearly said, "Them sons-of-bitches!" Shirley, a black waitress, materialized at my elbow, sobbing; though I would see many another tear shed, and would soon enough make my own salty contributions, she was the first person I saw crying on that stark and desperate day. "They shot him because he was *good,*" she sobbed.

Late that night, after a sad reunion with a congressman who had returned on the plane bearing President Kennedy's body from Dallas, I returned numbly home to join my countrymen in keeping the long TV vigil. At an hour I could not guess, my old friend Moe telephoned from Los Angeles.

"He didn't push for civil rights bills as much as many of us had hoped," he said. "Hell, I was criticizing him just last night. But goddammit, he sent federal marshals to Mississippi for James Meredith—and he federalized the National Guard to keep him there! He backed King up when he was in those fucking cracker jails. Black people thought that maybe here was one white man who understood. They thought maybe—oh shit, man, just compare the dude with old man Eisenhower!" I was among the thousands who streamed into the Capitol Rotunda to pay respects to our President as he lay in state. Though I have since heard numerous blacks proclaim JFK's deficiencies, they made up a high percentage of those waiting for hours in the cold, damp night; their grief appeared at least equal to that of white mourners.

On Sunday morning I went to my car to run an errand and discovered a flat tire. I had just begun struggling with the jack-stand, my cold fingers as blue and numb as the national mind, when a startlingly cheerful voice sang out, "Well, they got him."

I turned to regard a chunky black man who had more of joy and excitement than I had seen since the mesmerizing news from Dallas. He was hopping, skipping, almost dancing down the sidewalk.

"Beg your pardon?" I said.

"They got him! They got that Oswald!"

"What do you mean, they got him?"

"Some cat shot him in the belly," he said. "Walked right up and shot old Oswald's ass off."

"Jesus, are you sure?"

"Man, I just seen it on the box. They running it over and over."

I dropped the jackstand and ran toward my television set, yelling back, "How'd it happen? Who did it?"

"Man, I don't know," the black man said, "but I hope they give that cat a goddamn medal!"

# V
# On Through Mad Babylon

"I can hear you say, 'What a horrible, irresponsible bastard!' And you're right. I leap to agree with you. I am one of the most irresponsible beings that ever lived. Irresponsibility is part of my invisibility; any way you face it, it is a denial. But to whom can I be responsible, and why should I be, when you refuse to see me? And wait until I reveal how truly irresponsible I am. Responsibility rests upon recognition, and recognition is a form of agreement. Take the man whom I almost killed: Who was responsible for that near murder—I? I don't think so, and I refuse it. I won't buy it. You can't give it to me. *He* bumped *me, he* insulted *me.* Shouldn't he, for his own personal safety, have recognized my hysteria, my "danger potential"? He, let us say, was lost in a dream world. But didn't *he* control that dream world—which, alas, is only too real!—and didn't *he* rule me out of it? And if he had yelled for a policeman, wouldn't *I* have been taken for the offending one? Yes, yes, yes! Let me agree with you, I was the irresponsible one; for I should have used my knife to protect the higher interests of society. Some day that kind of foolishness will cause us tragic trouble. All dreamers and sleepwalkers must pay the price, and even the invisible victim is responsible for the fate of all."

—Ralph Ellison, *Invisible Man*

The assassin's bullets in Dallas shook up more heads than John F. Kennedy's alone, ripped through to the national psyche, bored to the national bone. After the initial shock many of us took new personal inventories and came away displeased. We had discovered spoiled goods: weevils in our mental bean bins, rats in our moral cheese. I have been amazed at the number of people who have since credited the traumas of a Presidential assassination with inspiring them to quit jobs or wives for which they could no longer find affection, or who otherwise dramatically changed their life styles. Even our politicians in their grief and guilt momentarily experienced a cleansing, Lyndon Johnson telling Congress "We shall overcome" and Congress itself passing the most meaningful of the civil-rights bills.

My own post-assassination verdict was that in a decade on Capitol Hill I had accomplished exactly nothing that might be claimed as satisfying or even marginally important. Like countless other young men who have deserted their native provinces for Washington, I arrived fueled more by raw enthusiasm and energy than by parliamentary knowledge or social skills—had somehow assumed to heal and build and save, to banish bureaucratic inefficiency, red tape, and injustice forever. Those vain dreams crashed in flames before the completion of a single two-year term as I encountered the hard realities of seniority politics, partisan politics, palsy-walsy politics in which the unwritten law among statesmen was that no personal applecarts should be tipped over. You preserve my obsolete Army base in the Umteenth District of California, Mister Chairman, and so long as the vote is taken in executive session (so that no public recording of it is made) I will act in that privacy to make it difficult for the nigger to vote in South Carolina. You vote against that insidious bill calling for a hairy congressional investigation into the gouging policies of the giant lending institutions, Charley, and come the next expensive re-election campaign I will point you in the direction of appreciative men of rare gifts. Go with the leadership on this one, Joe, and we'll give you that new post office or a better committee assignment or maybe a shot at the gubernatorial nomination back home.

As often happens with young would-be reformers, I ran out of crusading gases after encountering a certain number of endlessly frustrating hills. From there it was a short journey to becoming nothing more than a cynical hired hack. One did not immediately offer this confession to oneself, however. No, it was easier to imagine that some slow if invisible progress was being made in the Congressional institution and in the nation, even as one dictated responses to agitated mystics who would solve poverty by melting down the magnetic pole, or as one mailed out complimentary Agriculture Yearbooks with one's congressman's name stamped in bold letters everywhere the printer had permitted a blank space, or as one composed a series of speeches long on those safe clichés judged to be most popular with the general electorate or tailored to fit the prejudices of specific groups. After cynicism came boredom, then disgust, and finally shame; all encouraged drink or other forms of escapism, which may be why Capitol Hill temperatures always seemed to run about three degrees higher than the normal 98.6 degrees Fahrenheit. Long before President Kennedy's assassination, one had reached the point of doing not much more than going through the motions, becoming a creature about half robot and half clown. Though he could grind out the required bullshit press releases and weekly newsletters with his eyes closed, or answer constituent mail as evasively as the next fellow, he grew to live for the four-martini lunches that made his afternoons half bearable while waiting for the serious post-work revelry to begin.

These unpleasant turns required facing in the shaving glass, once the Kennedy trauma had first numbed and then slowly cleansed. One vowed to return to old priorities long ago abandoned. One would leave Congress to its petty vanities to resurrect an old goal, dream, ambition. One would write.

My new role encouraged frequent trips to New York's literary jungles in search of writing assignments or viable contacts. Here, in the great publishing houses of America, one looked about in the expectation that among men of letters that ole debbil bias surely had been put to rout. While publishers proudly listed the art of James Baldwin, Ralph Ellison, Richard Wright, John A. Williams, Chester Himes, or even wild LeRoi Jones, many houses as late as 1964 were continuing to publish only a relative handful of "Negro books" annually. And even after the explosion in "black writing" came, only those black authors who had earlier established their literary or political reputations likely were well blessed when it came to advance royalties or advertising budgets. Often, I felt, black writers received short shrift in the pages of most book-review sections: the reviews generally were written by comfortable white liberals whose values and experiences ill equipped them to judge books by men who took as their subjects life at the darkest point of the most bottomless social pits. And while one might occasionally encounter at cocktail parties the larger black literary names or black celebrities ranging from actor Brock Peters to singer Bobby Short to Boudini Brown (trainer for the young Muhammad Ali, and himself something of a mystic who wanted to write novels expressing some painful philosophy he could not easily articulate), one quickly discovered that black editors or executives remained in short supply.

Perhaps one found a higher degree of tolerance in publishing circles than had been uncovered in prior associations, though racist attitudes both malignant and benign sometimes revealed themselves. A top editor of one of America's oldest periodicals (now defunct) specialized when sober in dialect "nigger jokes"; drunk, he delivered mean-spirited anti-black tirades. Before he was through, he would balk at publishing stories even slightly sympathetic to black militants. A writer famed for his intellectualism described his personal distress when his teen-age daughter began dating a "schwartze": "Very well to proclaim one's self a loving liberal integrationist. The declaration is easily come by. But goddammit, something *chemical* happens to me when that black boy walks in the room. I see him returning with my grandchildren for Sunday dinners." I learned that a truly big-name writer, critically acclaimed and no stranger to the best-seller lists, apparently had the inability to carry on his personal correspondence without resorting to such terms as "boog," "jig," "Mau Maus," "niggers," or "dumb spades." Even worse, I occasionally found myself (for what I then assumed to be "professional reasons") pandering to his bigotry by responding in kind.

On writing assignments, one heard black people of whom one sometimes wrote recount their experiences in racist America —or "Mad Babylon," as Eldridge Cleaver views it. Ollie Matson, nearing the end of his professional football career with the Philadelphia Eagles, recalled the day in the 1950s when his San Francisco University team played an all-white team in Oklahoma: "I got hit with everything. Fist, elbows, knees. Finished that game with two black eyes, a bloody nose, and my face puffed up like pound cake. And you know what? I scored three touchdowns that day—and they were all called back." One does not think of the old jazz king, Louis Armstrong, as even mildly militant; more than one black has expressed the opinion that Armstrong inclines to "Tomism" or, as a Washington black, Julius Hobson, described him, "a good, happy black boy." I drank enough bourbon with "Pops" in private circumstances, however, to witness his inner rages as he talked of how in the old days white service-station operators ran to lock their rest rooms should a busload of black musicians pull up, of how white rowdies in whistle-stop towns chased down black musicians after dancing to their sounds "to beat on their asses with chains and cut 'em up with knives," of how "I played ninety-nine million hotels I couldn't stay at." ("If I had friends blowing at some all-white nightclub or hotel, I couldn't get in to see 'em—or them to see me. One time in Dallas, Texas,

some goddamn ofay stops me as I enter this hotel where I'm
blowing the show—me in a goddamn *tuxedo,* now!—and tells
me I got to come round to the back door. . . . Damn *right,* I'm
for the young dudes who ain't taking it no more. No man ought
to have to eat dirt.") Sugar Ray Robinson recalled that as a
young amateur he had so soundly defeated a promising young
white fighter in the latter's upstate New York home town that
he and his black manager were summarily jailed overnight
while agents of the defeated white fighter tried to prove Robinson a professional. Bubba Smith, the young All-Pro defensive
lineman with the Baltimore Colts, made all-American at Michigan State but later said, "I'm from Texas, just like you. I grew
up in Beaumont. My father coached the high-school team I
played on. Every big football school outside the deep South offered me scholarships—except in Texas, and that's where I
really wanted to play ball because Texas was home. But the
Texas schools couldn't use me. Maybe I clashed with their
school colors." Note that these examples come from the worlds
of show business and sports—areas where Whitey has always
particularly prided himself for the racial progress he has permitted.

Meanwhile, on visits back to Capitol Hill, one discovered
that one's departure from that scene had not immediately per-
fected the Congressional institution. Representative O. Clark
Fisher of, sad to say, Texas, orating against the voting-rights
bill of 1965, threw a verbal wild pitch in recalling "When Martin Luther King invaded Selma, Alabama, with its blood-splat-
tered demonstrations"—conveniently failing to note that the
demonstrators had provided the blood while Alabama "lawmen" and hooligans provided the splatter. When a bill came before the House to appropriate money to war on rats in the nation's slum cities, our legislators cracked bad jokes ("I say this
nonsense should end 'rat here and rat now' ") and otherwise enjoyed themselves before defeating the bill. One of the offenders,
Republican Joel Broyhill of Virginia's Tenth District, a million-
aire who represents a high percentage of federal employees who

flee the city at the end of each work day for their comfortable lily-white surburban bedroom communities, made a speech in late 1968 blasting the White House staff for having invited "three outspoken militants from the District of Columbia" to a meeting on educational goals. "I cannot believe that [the President] will get a true picture of this nation's goals from a group of bleary-eyed malcontents . . . all of whom have uttered declarations on public affairs which range from sabotage to revolution." These "bleary-eyed malcontents" included a young leader of Pride, Inc. (a federally subsidized group providing work-training programs for ghetto youth), a member of the D.C. school board, and a lady who served on a neighborhood planning council in the black ghetto.

In late 1964 and early 1965, I edited a small magazine, *Capitol Hill,* catering to the congressional scene and to its several thousand employees. Alarmed by congressional attempts to eliminate or reduce funds for D.C. Children's Hospital, playgrounds, libraries, orphanages, and other public institutions, our little magazine offered free transportation (and boatloads of publicity) to any congressman or senator who would take time personally to tour those institutions and view their desperate needs. I knew, from my old Hill experiences, that congressmen or senators who had troubled to inspect public facilities or services in the District were as rare as the swimming stone—even though Congress is charged with governing and funding the city. Though we hand-delivered our offer to all congressional offices, the only reaction we received came from a powerful staff bureaucrat in the Senate who barred our publication from circulation there on the grounds that it made trouble. And later, when the wretches of the Poor People's Campaign came to Washington to dramatize their plight by living in the shacks, tents, and mud of Resurrection City, far more legislators damned them in shrill or strident speeches than consented to receive them for an airing of their grievances.

When Watts exploded, in August of 1965, white Americans were unprepared. "What do they want?" we asked each other in front of our color television sets. "What are they *doing?*" Watts was unlike anything Americans remembered: the earlier, half-forgotten race riots in Detroit, Chicago, New York, and many other stations failed to fit the Watts pattern. Now blacks were burning what appeared, to white Americans, to be their own homes and stores. So blind was most of white America to ghetto conditions, so isolated and protected from the realities of the black slums, that we failed to realize how little even of their own squalor black people owned. As blacks used force against white citizens, white property, and even white policemen, we called it a riot—for that was the accepted term. But as we saw them stoning, torching, and looting while crying their chilling new slogan, "Burn, Baby, Burn," we must have known in our white hearts that it was something more: an insurrection, a revolt, a revolution. Who had expected, after all that cheek-turning, praying, and singing in the nonviolent civil-rights movement, back in a time when white Americans held a near-monopoly on racial violence, that blacks might one day fight back?

Elijah Muhammad's Black Muslims and the man known as Malcolm X had perhaps given the most serious public warnings to my generation that blacks would not forever turn the other cheek. When their messages first began to circulate in the white world, we were not immediately impressed. Elijah Muhammad and his followers were originally considered a source of mild amusement: just another nigger show that would eventually pass, like *Porgy and Bess,* or *Green Pastures* with its funny fish-fry scene and "De Lawd" strutting this way and that while breaking up poker games or potential fornications. Just another version of the Sleeping Car Porter's Ball with colorful costumes, elaborate titles, and comic or pretentious oratory. Why, everybody knew we weren't really "White Devils"—surely even the niggers knew better. Hadn't Lyndon Johnson himself said "We shall overcome"? Had not John F. Kennedy sprung Martin Luther King from a cracker jail or two? Had we not been nicey-nice to that young black couple we met at a dinner party in suburban Virginia six months ago? Did we not generously share our old clothes with our maids, or make an occasional contribution to the NAACP or donations to a black foundling home? Perhaps we judged Elijah Muhammad and Malcolm X along with Marcus Garvey or Father Divine (considered figures of fun in the white world), remembering Garvey for having paraded in purple sashes and an Admiral's hat while foolishly speaking of blacks going back to Africa by the boatload, and Father Divine for his confession that "Bein' God ain't no bed of roses."

Perhaps those of us who saw little fun in black-militant games found our old fears becoming unbolted, fears floating inside us like the darkest cargo. One defense for this discomfort was to judge black "extremists" as being more than slightly mad: and surely only a token handful would follow the lead of madmen. It was convenient to our peace of mind not to analyze what in our society might have driven significant numbers of black men mad (if, indeed, we insisted that such was their condition). It was likewise convenient, upon the assassination of Malcom X in February of 1965 not to see that act as a part of internal struggle among blacks for power and direction in a serious revolution, but to put it down as just another nigger killing inspired, perhaps, over who got to wear the flashier robes down at the lodge. If white Americans had any deep feelings for the assassinated black man, few manifested them. Indeed, I am of the mind that many white Americans sighed in relief at the permanent silencing of someone they considered a dangerous, crazy nigger.

Long after the assassination of Malcolm X, even such a gentle and basically Establishment figure as Dr. Martin Luther King continued to be reviled among whites as dangerous, subversive, or at best an uppity troublemaker. The FBI's eternal anachronism, J. Edgar Hoover, named him one of the world's outstanding liars. Lyndon Johnson and/or Robert Kennedy tapped his telephone, and somebody in Washington saw to it that his hotel or motel rooms were, when possible, electronically bugged. In the South, giant roadside billboards displayed a picture of Doctor King among those attending what was described as "a training session in a Communist school." If our statesmen did not think of Doctor King as "Red," they often considered him little more than a powerful demagogue with a huge bloc vote to be bartered. A popular "joke" on Capitol Hill, which I heard repeated more than once by congressmen, typified the latter view. "Bobby," Doctor King is alleged to have said as he walked along with Attorney General Robert Kennedy at his heels, "did you fart?" "Nosir," Kennedy quickly responds, "but I will if you want me to."

As Rap Brown, John Lewis, Stokely Carmichael, and other prideful black militants came on the scene with their tough talk and Afro influences, white Americans became increasingly uptight. Long before anyone in the white society had heard of Huey Newton, Bobby Seale, Eldridge Cleaver, or Black Panthers, Goldwater partisans were whispering of that hope residing in "white backlash," and George Wallace was reaping its benefits in such non-Dixie stations as Indiana, Baltimore, and Milwaukee. "Law and order" suddenly came to mean more than it formerly had. The frightened white man demanded it as a birthright, though law and order had not seemed so precious while all the lead was flying in one direction.

Even so perceptive, good, and hip a white man as Norman Mailer could write, in 1968, of his rawer emotions when irritated by being kept waiting for a press conference called by Dr. Ralph Abernathy to promote the Poor People's Crusade:

> . . . he [Mailer] was getting tired of Negroes and their rights. It was a miserable recognition, and on many a count, for if he felt even a hint this way, then what immeasurable tides of rage must be loose in America itself? . . . What an obsession was the Negro to the average white American by now. Every time that American turned in his thoughts to the sweetest object of contemplation in his mind's small town bower, nothing less than America the Beautiful herself—that angel of security at the end of every alley—then *there* was

the face of an accusing rioting Black right in the middle of the dream—smack in the center of the alley—and the obsession was hung on the hook of how to divide the guilt, how much to the white man, how much to the dark? . . . Was he stingier than he dreamed, more lacking in the true if exorbitant demand for compassion without measure . . . ?
 . . . He was weary to the bone of listening to Black cries of Black superiority in sex, Black superiority in beauty, Black superiority in war. . . . He was so heartily sick of listening to the tyranny of soul music, so bored with Negroes triumphantly late for appointments, so depressed with Black inhumanity to Black in Biafra, so weary of being sounded in the subway by Black eyes, so despairing of the smell of booze and pot and used-up hope and blood-shot eyes of Negroes bombed at noon, so envious finally of that liberty to abdicate from the long-year-end decade-drowning yokes of work and responsibility that he must have become in some secret part of his flesh a closet Republican—how else account for his inner, "Yeah man, yeah, go!" when fat and flatulent old Republicans got up in Convention Hall [at Miami] to deliver platitudes on the need to return to individual human effort?

White policemen, never famed for restraint among blacks, became even less mindful of the Constitutional niceties under the warm influence of Whitey's increasing resentments. My friend Davis Carter, a white Episcopal minister and former Capitol Hill associate, learned shortly after moving into a Washington area where blacks predominate how differently the police operated from the way they had in the all-white Virginia community where he had previously lived. One night shortly after Davis and his wife, Mary, had moved into an old house they were painstakingly renovating, they were startled by shotgun-bearing policemen bursting into their home through all available doors—battering down those that did not readily respond to gentler pressures. The officers stopped short, nonplused at the sight of a white couple in the territory. Their stammered explanation: they were seeking a certain police character, a nigger, who was thought to be in the neighborhood, and, sorry folks, ha-ha, we can see he wouldn't be *here*. "Do you have warrants to search these homes?" the Carters demanded. The police did not: obviously shotguns and battering rams served the purpose of legally executed search warrants where black homes were the targets of official suspicions. The "quick-entry" or "no-knock" law passed recently by Congress was, significantly, aimed at the District of Columbia— statistically the nation's blackest city.

After Watts and other insurrections, I heard many whites reassure themselves in Washington or its nervous suburbs that "it can't happen here." With the President and Congress in residence, provisions surely had been made to protect the Capitol; a single Molotov cocktail would bring thousands of riot-trained policemen and paratroopers. Washington Negroes had decent government jobs and therefore wouldn't fall prey to outside agitators or professional militants.

These graveyard whistlings ignored several near-misses: the sacking of Glen Echo Amusement Park (segregated for years after other Washington institutions had bowed to the inevitable); a mini-riot at D.C. Stadium during a game for the city football championship; countless skirmishes between ghetto blacks and their police tormentors; inflammatory racist speeches in the halls of Congress; dozens of instances where black toughs had attacked whites driving through the rowdier and more hopeless sections of Anacostia, Southeast, or Northeast Washington. Washingtonians read these reports and refused to believe. No amount of black unrest or nonviolent protest over degrading requirements attending welfare benefits (the "man-in-the-house rule," not outlawed by the Supreme Court until early 1970, precluded assistance to any family with an adult male in the house, thus leaving some unemployed or only marginally employed black men no choice but to quit their families), no number of violent crimes or demonstrations against police harassments or protests against ill-equipped and de facto segregated schools, could make it clear to whites that the black man had had enough. Only "agitators" and "troublemakers" were discontent, the prevailing sociology ran, and things were getting better for the black man every day: why, look at Thurgood Marshall, Carl Rowan, James Brown, Gayle Sayers. I was never able to convince anyone that we lived in a fool's paradise.

For I had become (for the first time since my invasion of hostile Harlem many years before) sorely afraid of the black man. I had seen his growing hostility, not only in the more miserable slums where I had occasionally gone to perform a bleeding-heart good deed or two (helping to keep slum playgrounds open when Congress threatened to close them, or other such stopgap gestures), but in the whole of the city. Within a stone's throw of Hubert Humphrey's plush high-rise, with its stunning view of the Potomac and green Virginia fields, I had incurred the wrath of a black street gang by unwisely attempting to rescue a small black boy in the process of being robbed of his pocket change—and had paid for my rashness by having to steer my wife through bawled invitations to inventive fornications. I have no doubt that had it not been broad daylight, and in an affluent precinct more than nominally patrolled by cruising police cars, that additional vengeance would have been extracted from my meddling white hide.

I had been the handy object of rock-throwing bands of small Negro boys, none surely above the age of ten, who chose me as the target of their frustrations near our neighborhood shopping center. When I drove a black woman to her home in a scabby section at the end of her work day as our weekly domestic, carrying a box of clothing she had gratefully received as a gift up several flights of foul-smelling stairs, her young daughter had fixed me with a glare of pure hate and the lip-curling thanks of "Shit!" Following Louis Armstrong on a writing assignment, my wife and I made a tour of nightclubs with Armstrong's trombonist, the merry and talented Tyree Glenn, and Mrs. Glenn. Tyree and I were more or less alternately picking up the series of bar tabs. In one joint, about three o'clock in the morning, we struggled over a check until a black man on a neighboring stool instructed Glenn, "Man, let Whitey pay. *Always* let Whitey pay. The cocksucker can pay till Christmas and he *still* owe us." There was the other extreme. Out of old guilts, compassion, expediency—who knows?—I became so generous in small coins to bands of young black beggars that I became known to them as "The Money Man": a mark, a John, Big Whitey, a target for increasing demands, hustles, put-ons, and condescending attitudes.

Time after time in Washington stores I had seen young blacks be rude, threatening, obscene, or violent to white customers and clerks. I understood why such things happened (having seen the other side of the coin throughout my life), but where I had once walked the streets in confidence, I came to look ahead like a soldier advancing into enemy territory, alert for unfriendly blacks or side-street dangers, vulnerable, tense, and marked—at last—by my white skin. Yes, the world was being turned around; chickens were coming home to roost. Meanwhile, at cocktail parties in segregated living rooms, I would hear the many reasons why "it can't happen here."

On a warm, rain-threatened evening in April of 1968, some four years after I had quit politics, an old friend with whom I had served Capitol Hill time telephoned my Washington home: "Have you heard what happened to Martin Luther King?"

I knew as surely as an eyewitness: "Oh, goddamn! Somebody shot the poor son-of-a-bitch!"

"The lid will blow now," I said. "Especially if he dies. They'll burn it all down." Within a short time Doctor King's death was confirmed. I called my friend back, noting his excellent White House connections while I currently was in bad odor there: he should contact a mutual friend on LBJ's staff and beg that all possible conciliatory gestures be made—a shutdown of business operations, all manner of pledges to employ unlimited federal power in bringing the assassin to justice, the President's promise to attend the funeral service or a promise to transport the body to wherever Mrs. King might choose. Though these might be no more than empty gestures compared to the horror of the foul murder, they were no less than the black community had a right to expect. (Three years earlier, when Malcolm X had been killed, it had not occurred to me that any official gestures of condolences might be appropriate from white leaders.)

My friend called back within the hour: "They're reserving Sunday as the official day of mourning. Businesses will be closed and everything."

Was that all?

"Yes."

"Well, fuck that! It's not enough. Most businesses are closed on Sunday, anyway. Dammit, they've got to do something meaningful. Otherwise, it will be construed as an insult."

"They seem to think they know what they're doing over there," my friend said. "The President's going on TV here in a little bit and tell everybody to simmer down."

"Isn't that ducky? I suppose he'll recommend that we should all sit and reason together, and that's supposed to cool it."

Though we did not know it then, the first plate-glass windows were being kicked in on 7th Street and along 14th Street in the heart of the black ghetto. ("The primary riot corridors," our newspapers would designate them.)

Through most of a sleepless night I listened to the radio, picking up reports of violence and random burnings. Near dawn I fell into a drugged sleep, awaking in midmorning when my brother, Weldon, telephoned from Texas to see if we were safe. "Sure," I said, groggy and puzzled. "Why?"

"You'd better wake up," he said. "Your town is on fire. I'm watching it on television."

From my yard I could see puffy clouds of smoke in Washington's betrayed and hopeless sections. I tuned in a talk show on a surburban radio station: whites, imitating the fiddling Nero, bitched because government flags would be flown at half-mast for the fallen black leader. ("After all, he wasn't a government official.") Or they accused Senator Robert Kennedy of grandstanding for political gain in having ordered his private plane to fly the body back to Atlanta for burial. More than one hundred American cities were burning; machine guns protected Capitol Hill; nightly curfews were announced; National Guard troops camped in the schoolyard across the street from my apartment, and were visible in Hubert Humphrey's block a few hundred yards away. One remembered a line by Richard Wright: "The machine gun on the corner is the symbol of the twentieth century."

Late Saturday night, someone knocked on my door. Through the peephole I saw two well-dressed black men. Though ashamed of myself, I decided for safety's sake not to answer. As they turned away, one laughed and spoke to the other about Whitey being afraid to come out of his hole.

Near midnight there were sirens in the neighborhood, and the sounds of gunshots. I keep no firearms, but that night Whitey, the son of the night watchman, slept with a billy club fashioned from a broomstick and a wicked butcher knife next to his bed.

Harvard. Surely that bastion of reason, that sunny intellectual garden in a mindless world of thorns, would prove to be one place in America where racial bigotry was not clearly visible. Surely Harvard was far too gentlemanly, Cambridge much too cosmopolitan, New England much too proper, to permit the wild flowering of thoughtless prejudices. On arriving in September of 1969 to begin a year as a Nieman Fellow, I remember thinking that perhaps in that academic community, representing the northernmost geographical point of my American meanderings, I would find respite from those old divisions and hatreds which increasingly had rent and crippled my country.

America's race relations, I thought, had touched the decade's bottoming-out point. Promises by our politicians to rebuild the nation's charred ghettos—promises made out of fear and shock following upheavals triggered by Doctor King's assassination —simply had not been kept: one could drive along the primary riot corridors in Washington and see hopeless blacks sitting among the scorched and aging ruins, see the same clots of street dudes waiting with sullen faces on corners where Whitey might drive by in search of day laborers, see the same winos and con men and street urchins drinking or scheming or cursing without change. The Kerner Commission's report affirming the obvious (that America was truly two nations, one white and one black, one fat and one hungry, one free and one not) had proved so displeasing to the President who ordered it that Lyndon B. Johnson had locked it away virtually without official comment. The assassination of Senator Robert Kennedy had removed the last white politician trusted by many blacks. As it became clear to black Americans that despite pious newspaper editorials and rosy political promises their lot would not soon be bettered, militancy increased across the board. White America became as extraordinarily fearful of the Black Panthers as it had been of domestic Communists in the 1950s, though in neither case did either group have the numerical strength or resources to justify the majority's hysteria. Just as in the McCarthy era little or no distinction was made between "liberals" and Communists, so all blacks who expressed dissatisfaction with the racist society were too often lumped into the Black Panther bag.

Even old friends who had once been active in civil-rights demonstrations confessed new feelings of fear, rejection, resentment. "I'm tired of being called a honky bastard," one of them said in his comfortable Manhattan apartment. "Those people aren't making distinctions between us and the rednecks any more." The suggestion that white Americans now saw virtually all blacks as looters or revolutionaries was not well received by my old friend: he was reluctant to admit that both sides had polarized, not merely the blacks. One sensed that white America, like the night watchman's son in the wake of Doctor King's assassination, slept behind locked doors and with weapons near at hand. Still, some remaining vestiges of a fool's optimism led me to expect the best at Harvard.

On that September day when we sixteen Fellows met for our introductory luncheon in the Harvard Faculty Club, an academic graybeard called one of our two black members aside to confide what marvelous opportunities the black Niemans had to provide inspiration by "setting good examples." Each of those black men held college degrees, one having graduated with honors from an Ivy League school. Each had almost a decade behind him as a competent and responsible journalist; both had spotless records as good citizens in the way those things are conventionally judged. Yet, for all of this, the old Harvard geezer somehow felt they deserved special exhortations; somehow presumed he had a right, possibly a duty, to visit on them insulting lectures he would not dare offer to any white man who walked in to repair the soft-drink machine.

I encountered one couple who never before had eaten at the same table with blacks; others in that community of letters had known this simple experience only as it had been forced upon them in a military messhall or at some public function. One of my fellow Niemans, who for weeks had represented himself as free of racial bias, began one conversation, "King, you're our nigger expert, so tell me: what do they want?" Another Nieman drunkenly referred to one of our black colleagues, in his presence, as "our house nigger." Over cocktails in the home of a man whose face is known in the highest Harvard staff councils, my wife and I heard how the Cambridge-Boston area had gone to hell due to "a rising colored population now approaching seventeen per cent."

White America's official and brutal disregard for black futures was becoming increasingly apparent as I arrived in Cambridge; by the time I departed, in June of 1970, I would see evidence that black hopes had crashed to their lowest point in more than a decade. And why not? For there had been, by then, an obvious and systematic war of genocide against the Black Panthers, their leaders killed in their beds, sent into exile, or imprisoned under excessive bonds of $100,000 per man so as to preclude even their temporary freedom. One stared blankly and spiritlessly at the television set or newspaper headlines as events revealed themselves, sometimes wondering if, after all, George Wallace had won the Presidency. Attorney

General John Mitchell attempted to substitute a watered-down version for the tough 1965 voting-rights act, inspiring sixty-five of seventy-four Justice Department lawyers in the Civil Rights Division to demand reassurances of good faith on the part of the Nixon Administration. "It seems to me there are two extreme groups," the President would say at a press conference. "There are those who want instant integration and those who want segregation forever. I believe that we need to have a middle course between those two extremes. That's the course on which we are embarked." One wondered what such nonsense meant: would we have instant integration at some point about halfway between here and "forever," or would we forever have creeping desegration?

For the first time in almost twenty years the Justice Department *opposed* racial integration in certain Southern school districts, and President Nixon attempted to make gifts to the Supreme Court of Judges Clement Haynsworth of South Carolina and G. Harold Carswell of Florida. Martha Mitchell placed her midnight call to an Arkansas newspaper to recommend that a United States senator be "crucified" for his opposition to the Carswell nomination. Federal agents failed to intervene when whites beat with chains and toppled South Carolina school buses loaded with black children. No protest was heard from the White House when Mississippi highway patrolmen, returning nonexistent "sniper fire," fired fatal shots into black student dormitories at Jackson State, or when six blacks in Augusta, Georgia, died with police slugs in their backs. Policemen on trial for their parts in the Algiers Motel incident in Detroit, where three blacks had been killed and others brutalized during the 1967 riots, were acquitted to the applause and cheers of white spectators.*

As these sorry events unfolded, one saw in Cambridge evidence of mounting black anger. It is axiomatic that the more disenchanted blacks grow with white society, the more aggres-

---

* The shocking facts of this case are presented in John Hersey's *The Algiers Motel Incident,* published in 1968 by Knopf, New York.

sively they seek identification with the roots of black culture. Over the months at Harvard one noted that numerous blacks replaced their former clipped styles with Afro or "natural" hair growths; white shirts, ties, and jackets were replaced by the blue denims favored in the Poor People's Crusade, or by para-military shirts or berets copied from the Black Panthers, or by dashikis or African-styled robes. Increasing, the black students of Harvard and their white colleagues went their separate ways. "Two years ago black students associated themselves with our social or political actions," a white senior said, "but more and more they withdraw into their own action groups." This trend is particularly distressing when one considers that more racial rapport—or, at least, fewer racial hostilities—traditionally occur among the young than among their elders. When I at-tempted to enroll in a black-studies course, the instructor bluntly said that his students had voted against whites' being enrolled on the grounds that their presence would impede full and frank discussions. "Don't you think I could take it?" I de-manded. "No," the instructor said with a slight smile. "Look," he added, "I could teach a black history course sugar-coated for whites, but it would be too goddamn elementary for my black students. *They* don't have to have the problem explained to them." One noted the close fraternity among blacks, exhibited in strangers calling each other "Brother" and "Sister" without apparent regard to social or economic considerations.

Several of our Nieman dinner seminars revealed worsening stresses between blacks and whites. These were evenings when we attempted to balance racially our discussion panels, and our audiences, in search of "meaningful dialogues": we hoped for hope, at least, if not for definitive answers. Liquor flowed freely at these confrontations, which may have been wiser than strict prohibitionists would care to admit: if the flow did not assist reason, it at least encouraged candor. In such circumstances a noted professor of government and social relations was not per-mitted to get away with his bald declaration that the black man was merely taking his turn at the bottom of the sociological barrel, that the Irishman had been there, and the Italian in his turn, and the Jew in his, so that once the black man had served his apprenticeship he would know a routine rising on democracy's rich gases. Hisses and boos properly greeted such simplistic reasoning, which ignored among other basics a two-hundred-and-twenty-five-year history of slavery followed by several decades of restrictions *by law* as well as by custom— conditions never duplicated in the case of the Irishman, the Italian, or the Jew.

"But what can *I* do?" a white Nieman wailed to black panelists. "I'm just one insignificant little white newspaper man. What can I really do to help?" "Aw, man, don't give us that shit," a black man snapped. "We've heard it all our lives." Blacks shouted their approval, while whites shook their heads as if to say *How sad to be rejected when one comes in good faith!* "Things can't be too bad," one white cheerfully said, "because three or four years ago there were no black Niemans and *you* wouldn't have been eating in the Harvard Faculty Club." That he went uncheered for this insight seemed to surprise the fellow.

One evening Dr. Ewart Guinier, chairman of the Afro-American Studies Department, condemned white liberals at Harvard who had sat idly as blacks made their pioneer fights for black-studies programs and job opportunites. Adam Yarmolinsky, former advisor to President Kennedy and then a professor in the Harvard Law School (who, ironically, had been drummed out of the Pentagon by congressional neanderthals who suspected him because they had difficulty pronouncing his name), shocked the assembly by saying, "Doctor Guinier, all that you have said in the last ten minutes makes you unfit to be a member of the Harvard faculty." Hissed and cat-called, Professor Yarmolinsky shouted, *"Do you know who I am?"* "No," one white Nieman taunted, "who are you?" The professor told us, gratuitously adding, "Robert Kennedy understood black people better than any man in America."

"How can you say that?" his Nieman tormentor challenged.

"All right, so Robert Kennedy tried, so he was growing. But don't try to pass him off as the know-all see-all. I remember when he called together a very successful and relatively tame group of blacks to his Manhattan apartment—people such as Harry Belafonte, Lena Horne, James Baldwin, Sidney Poitier —to hip him to black complaints. He got resentful as hell, man, when they laid a little heavy truth on him."

"Are you telling me Senator Kennedy was *against* blacks?" Yarmolinsky demanded.

"No, but I'm telling you that while Bobby Kennedy may have been in a state of becoming, he had not yet *become*."

One cannot, it develops, safely denigrate a Kennedy on Harvard soil. The meeting dissolved into a shouting match. Two white Niemans, who did not think ill of one another, mutually approached the bar. "I've had it with this shit," the first said. "I'm sick of doing the masochistic guilt bit. My old man was an immigrant who spoke no English, and he worked his way up from a pushcart to educate a big family. I don't want to hear this 'disadvantaged' horseshit."

"You dumb son-of-a-bitch," his learned colleague said, "you remind me of the French Cajun who bragged about getting elected to the Louisiana State Senate despite his 'racial handicap.' Don't give me any of your simple-minded, boot-strap-immigrant examples, unless you can show me that your old man had a black ass. He didn't, and therefore your story only reaffirms America's sickness." Cooler heads prevented violence, though not before harm was done to a budding friendship.

"I've spoken to my last white audience," a black man from the New Boston Urban League said at the conclusion of one such evening. "I don't have the strength any more to play their games. They come here thinking they're full of brotherhood, and the more they drink and the more truth they hear the more they come on like vigilantes." "God," said another black man visiting from Washington, "if Harvard professors and big-time journalists are this goddamned bigoted, where's all the racial progress I read about in the *New York Times*?"

At one dinner seminar the commanding general of an Army base bragged to his table companions of unusual democracy attendant to his organization. No racial bias, he said, spoiled his command. (And, indeed, a black friend had earlier told me that the general was as free of racial bias as any military man he had known, laughingly adding, "For that matter, he's better than most Harvard professors I have known.") The general's declaration, however, was more than his integrated dinner companions could accept without challenge.

What was the black-white ratio under the general's command?

"Oh, we have units with as low as eleven percentum blacks, and units with as high as forty-six percentum."

And what unit held the eleven percentum, General?

"Well, ah, the Command unit. Headquarters."

Uh-huh. And what unit held the forty-six percentum?

"Well, that unit is composed of service troops."

And how would you define "service troops," General?

"Well, you know—truck drivers, supply personnel, orderlies, cooks and bakers, housekeeping personnel. . . ."

Knowing laughter swept all tables where blacks remained within earshot, and someone shouted *Right on, General!* before someone else remarked that conditions had not changed a goddamn bit since 1948. From that point on, the Army's contribution to an integrated evening concentrated on his medium-rare filet.

Thick residues of bitterness and despair remained in both black and white camps after these experiences. One evening I accompanied a mixed group, about sixty-forty black, to the home of my fellow Nieman, Wally Terry of *Time,* after a particularly rough confrontation between the races. There a young black man, hearing that I was writing a book to be called *Confessions of a White Racist,* sneered and berated me for my exploitations. When I walked unexpectedly into a room where two black men were holding an animated conversation, they shifted gears as abruptly and obviously as if I had entered wearing the robes of a Ku Kluxer and carrying a bullwhip. A young black woman challenged me to reveal "what you whites really say about us" in private circumstances, and when I obliged an uproar ensued. Late in the evening the host whispered in my ear, "Say, man, I'm gonna tell the gray cats to cut —all except you. To hell with all this hostility! When they're gone, we can party with the Brothers." I momentarily felt myself in the presence of the highest compliment. Then floods of doubt and confusion drove the warm feeling away. "No," I said, "that's acting too much like the other side. You can't do that, Wally." "That may be," my host said immediately. "Do you think I really care?"

Caring. Appearances. Conditioned reflexes. They dominate. After I had become friendly with a young black woman, to whose home in the Roxbury section of Boston I had originally gone in the company of Wally and Janis Terry, there to discover my white face to be one of perhaps five among seventy-odd black ones, she confessed her reaction on first hearing my stubborn Texas accent: "What the hell is that cracker doing in *my* house?" On several social occasions it became necessary for Wally Terry to assure black people, "This dude has his head together." Though his recommendations did not always promote fast or lasting friendships, they doubtlessly opened doors that otherwise would have remained closed.

Whites, too, had their automatic up-tight reactions. Following our racial confrontations at the Harvard Faculty Club my white associates were alternately stunned, outraged, or skeptically amused at what they had heard. Some were honestly angry, feeling that blacks had gone beyond the artistic pale in attacking author William Styron to his face for his alleged misuse of historical material in writing *The Confessions of Nat Turner;* others accused our black guests of excessive emotionalism or of rude racisms of their own. Perhaps a majority, however, preferred to believe they had attended some harmless extension of Genet's *The Blacks*—had witnessed nothing more than theatrics meant to make the white man cringe a mite in payment of his first-class ticket and smooth sweet ride. One of our Niemans perfectly expressed this attitude: "Come on, now, don't you think they're exaggerating a bit for our benefit? Aren't they taking advantage of our white guilt to put us on? Come on, now."

One does not doubt that blacks have played roles for fun and profit amidst the racial confusions of an America seeking itself, an America groping and confused, for one has seen convincing performances among so-called militants who take money or position in exchange for hornswoggling frightened white organizations into the comfortable belief they are helping to "cool it" in the streets. There are, indeed, hip dudes who prey on Whitey: self-appointed "black leaders" who have no followers, "spokesmen" who speak only for themselves and who go off to count their profits while laughing behind their hands. I have known some few of these, both in the flesh and from newspapers or television. They are con men, pure and simple, even with the weight of basic morality on their side. To assume that all blacks, however, are merely playing games is to misread events at our peril. The men who came before our Nieman group had long-established credentials as concerned, erudite, dedicated blacks active in politics, the academic world, street protests, and such conventional organizations as the Urban League, National Association for the Advancement of Colored People, and the church. I did not spot a frivolous man among them, from the most soft-spoken to the most militant. One marveled at the protective persistence of his white associates as they attempted to explain away black anger, black frustrations, black warnings of the fire next time.

Perhaps my companions would not have remained so complacent had they spent time in the private company of some of our black guests. Men like C. Sumner "Chuck" Stone (author, television commentator, educator, former assistant to Congressman Adam Clayton Powell); Melvin King of the New Boston Urban League; Roger Wilkins (former Assistant Attorney General to Ramsey Clark in the Johnson Administration, and now a

Ford Foundation executive; Doctor Guinier of the Harvard faculty; Jerry Cox of the Harvard Medical School; Edward Sylvester, former Assistant Secretary, HEW; Howard E. Mitchell, professor of urbanism, University of Pennsylvania; Cleveland Sellers (a former student leader wounded in the Orangeburg, South Carolina, massacre of 1968); Haywood Henry of Boston (a chemist who doubles as a black-studies instructor at Harvard) —these and others made it clear, without histrionics, that they and other black Americans have had just about enough.

Perhaps my associates might have trembled had they heard the hours and hours of tapes Wally Terry had gathered in Vietnam, where for two years he was a foreign correspondent, for a book on the attitudes of black soldiers. I listened through many a wintry Cambridge night, hearing the anger, despair, profanities, threats. Blacks of all conditions and of varied military rank and experiences told of routine racisms encountered, of maltreatment at the hands of their white comrades-in-arms, from their officers, from, indeed, their government. "Man," said one volcanic dude, "they tell the Brothers they can't wear Afro hair, you dig, because it ain't regulation. But them white crackers wear sideburns down to their asses, like they was in the Confederate Army or something. And they say we can't give the Black Power salute among the Brothers, see, but yet Whitey can fly his fucking Confederate flag, man, and nobody says shit. Well, to hell with that flag. That flag means slavery to me."

No, another black voice said in detached irony, he did not expect to find improvements on returning to America, unless all the whites had somehow caught cholera and died. "Some Brothers dig on beast chicks"—meaning white girls—another said, "but how can that beast chick's head be where mine's at when she don't know what it is to hustle a hot dog for breakfast, man, or a stale sweet roll, man? Say she's dating a beast cat and wants to groove on dinner or the movies—he can take her out, man, 'cause the white dude's got a decent job; he's got bread.

She's dating *me* and wants to fly high—hell, we got to put it in the budget! So how's she gonna dig my blackness enough to make it with me?"

And another voice: "The Man stripped Cassius Clay of his title when Clay said he was a Muslim, right? And when he said he didn't have nothing against the Cong, the Man sentenced him to jail. I got nothing against the Cong, if you want to get it on —man, he's colored too. *He* could be a Brother." And still another: "Yeah, well, all my people's been janitors and like that, see, never had nothing. Never asked for nothing. I'm gonna ask. And then if I don't get what's mine, I'm gonna *take*." "LBJ?" one black soldier asked, laughing. "I didn't have nothing against the cat—tell you the truth, I liked him, I mean, you *knew* he was gonna come on television and have 'a heavy hort.' Hell, man, that was his hustle. [Laughs.] Nixon? Nixon sucks! Nixon eats it, man!"

Black soldiers spoke bitterly of crosses burned in Vietnam, of GIs cursed as "black bastards . . . jigaboos . . . niggers," of soul music not permitted by white platoon leaders who preferred to hear "hillbilly shit," of blacks sent on dangerous combat missions while whites draw less hazardous duty all out of proportion to prevailing racial ratios, of how little attention the military's internal race war has received in the American press, of politicians who have no concern for black futures, of how change is coming, goddammit, one way or another. No, I doubt whether many contented souls at Harvard would have assumed a gigantic black put-on had they listened night after night to those chilling outpourings of rage.

Wally and Janis Terry's three children, ranging from ages three to seven, remembered little of America after more than two years in Southeast Asia. "Little Wally didn't know what it was to be called a nigger until he got back here," his father said one evening, "but you can be damn sure they're teaching him." One night I called at the Terry home to find the household in a blue mood. Little Wally had been roasted for his color by his tiny schoolmates on that given day, and as the only black child in his class he felt particularly alone. He came home in an uncharacteristic mood, silent and pensive, and had ultimately been discovered listening to Aretha Franklin records with tears on his cheeks. There had followed a painful conversation between father and son, Wally Terry attempting to make sense of racial insanities exactly as I had attempted thirteen years earlier with my own small daughter when she learned of the racist bombing of a Tennessee school. Later, my black friend put on another of the Vietnam tapes, and we heard again the angry spewings of desperate and hopeless men. I looked at Janis (a lovely woman who grew weary in Cambridge of saying No, she was not Vietnamese, she was not Chinese, she was not Eurasian, she was black), a native of the District of Columbia, a former school teacher from a solidly middle-class black family, a mother whose mind and heart hurt that evening because her son had come home pathetically bewildered over why he should be reviled as "a dirty little nigger." It was a day, given her own experiences in a racist society, that she must have always known would come—a day she must have thought of long in advance of its arrival, with God-knows-what in her mind as she awaited it. The sure knowledge that it would come, however, surely made it no more acceptable or any less injurious. As she heard black soldiers speaking from Vietnam their bitter vows of better days, and of extracting whatever overdue vengeance they might find necessary, there was an almost ethereal glow on her face, a bright mad saintly beauty. She touched her husband's arm, smiling. "Baby," she said, softly, "guess who's coming home?"

These final lines are written from an ocean-front cottage in Maryland, just a mile or so below the Mason-Dixon line. The weather is hot and gasping, no matter that the calender attests to late September 1970. Hundreds of people enjoy the sun, sea, and surf. They come from Washington and Baltimore, from Delaware and from Maryland's Eastern Shore, from enclaves in New Jersey, Pennsylvania, and New York. For a week my wife and I have toured the several miles of beach, seeing no blacks other than those waiting on our tables, making our beds, or hauling away our trash. No one apparently finds this remarkable.

A few miles from here, in towns named Easton, Salisbury, Denton, and Dover, racial violence has become a common summer occurence. This month the newspapers tell of recent shoot-outs between policemen and black militants in Philadelphia, New Orleans, and Chicago. Washington, approximately two hours away by car, has known three consecutive nights of street battles, looting, and torchings. I see no concern on white faces turned upward to darken in the sun. I hear no alarm expressed on the beaches, in the restaurants or cocktail lounges or amusement parks. One is astonished at how quickly the human animal adjusts to catastrophe and chaos as part of the norm. Five years ago we sat in front of our television sets, alternately perplexed and frightened and angry, wondering what those crazy bastards in Watts were trying to prove. Now we listen with only one ear to reports of the latest battles in a war that is rapidly becoming our national open secret, or we switch the dial to catch the college football scores.

Our newspapers and television commentators play these battles down more than formerly. Racial insurrections are by this time old hat. Skyjackings complete with hostages provide the big news of the day, along with reports of a Russian submarine base being constructed in Cuba, and Spiro Agnew reading on the campaign stump from Doctor Spock's book on how to raise babies in a fool's effort to explain why America has become unbolted. The Vice-President, and the rest of us, may stick our heads in the sand; it will not, however, change the fact that America in the 1970s is in the midst of a domestic race war.

Armed confrontations between militant blacks and police have steadily increased, each side becoming progressively more self-righteous in its indignation, more harsh in its rhetoric, more deadly behind the gun. Little in the national air or in the national experience foretells a lessening of racial tensions. In the absence of corrective influences, human events—like stones rolling downhill—tend to progress at increasing speeds in the direction in which they are headed. Witness, as example, Vietnam. Logic dictates that a racial Armageddon awaits the American future.

Far too many white Americans and white institutions are failing to change in a time when change is required as the only viable alternative to an escalation of the race war. Since confrontations and the *desire* for confrontations are proceeding apace among those who daily and most directly establish the battlefield pace—policemen and militant blacks—while helpful reforms or conciliatory attitudes lag far behind, more statistical opportunities are provided for a racial Armageddon than are offered to avoid it. Our society has guaranteed that the most unimaginative of men shall police us, by providing them a rung near the bottom of the socio-economic ladder. It is these men, often ill-trained and almost always under-educated or pathetically lacking in the basic psychological skills, who almost exclusively represent the white world in the black ghetto.

By word and deed, we have taught our policemen that they exist primarily to protect property and men of property. They have observed in our courts that the black man historically has been dealt with more harshly than has the white offender. In society at large they have observed the black man's social, economic, and political ostracization. Little wonder that these men of generally limited gifts and frightening responsibilities imitate their political and social superiors when the opportunity is presented, for they desire nothing so much as upward mobility, a chance to gain that solid middle-class respectability, order, and economic security long represented to them as vital components of the American Dream. They are not sophisticated enough to realize that ghetto blacks do not live among rats, garbage, junkies, and welfare lines by choice so much as by the circumstances to which they—and their ancestors—were born. They know only that cousin Salvatore or brother-in-law Casey or old friend Smith rose from modest beginnings through hard work and perseverance to command their own law offices, real-estate firms, or gas stations. Why, then, can't Willie or Roosevelt do the same? The easy answer is that blacks lack ambition, or ability, rather than equal opportunity. Such handy conclusions breed a volatile mixture of white contempt, fear, and smug supremacy. When many of our white politicians pander to public fears through scare campaigns, or when social or political units continue to evade Supreme Court desegregation decisions almost twenty years old, or when our President fails to offer even a morality lecture in opposition to well-publicized brutalities against the black minority, what can the white policeman believe other than that he is proceeding on a true course?

The white policeman (like many other white Americans) fails to understand that he who has been constantly brutalized will, in time, become something of a brute himself: it is a matter of simple survival, of accommodating necessity, of, indeed, obeying the laws of evolution and the rule of environment. Whites, never having been subjected to the routine authoritarianisms of policemen hardened to the ghetto or to the daily injustices of the poorer streets, cannot understand why, at a given point, the black man might find a solution of sorts in reaching for the gun. They cannot understand the inner satisfaction a black man might feel in throwing a brick through the window of a loan-shark firm guilty of having robbed his family for generations, or the sweet surge of new power a black man might experience in seeing a honky cop brought down in the same unfeeling manner a black brother or cousin or father had been brought down by white authority a week or a year or a generation ago. People who are comfortable, or free—or who think themselves free—cannot possibly understand the workings of the revolutionary mind or the satisfaction to be found in simple vengeance. They do not know what it is for the brain to burn or the blood to boil in such righteous outrage that there are considerations more precious than life itself, for they cannot fathom what it is to have nothing to lose and everything to gain. They cannot imagine what it would be to look in the mirror some morning and decide that the time has come to determine whether one really has balls or guts or desperation enough to fight against great odds for his children's future.

Our policemen, servants to the system and feeling a natural affinity to the powerful white world that has commissioned them to carry badges and guns, are blinded to everything save carrying out the king's mission. In their view they are soldiers of the king: it becomes their simple duty to war on any who would threaten the palace, its conventional wisdoms, or traditional values. All too often they fail to make distinctions between the armed robber and the street-corner idler, or to judge the unruly drunk independently of the angry welfare mother demonstrating for a better deal for her family. These men we send into the tinder boxes of our interior cities (which we, in increasing numbers, flee for the white suburbs) to police a culture they neither understand nor approve. Once there, they daily encounter black people no more sophisticated, no more tolerant, no better educated than themselves—people who hate and fear the police as deeply as they are themselves hated and feared. Tell me a better way to promote war.

Let us not believe that black people have only recently come to mistrust and despise the white man, nor find comfort in the nonsense that a few Communists, professional agitators, or special crazies are the cause of our new trouble. Blacks have long known our low opinion of them, for we have made it clear over three hundred years, and their hearts have reciprocated for generations: they are simply manifesting their feelings in more open and direct ways, and with more of a final desperation. We should not think that the clock will somehow turn itself back. There are teen-age blacks in America who remember nothing of the Uncle Tom days, who have never shuffled and grinned in the white man's presence and who never will. In Cambridge last year I knew a three-year-old black boy named David who attacked and kicked a television repairman who called on his home, simply because the intruder was white. In Washington ten days ago, on the grounds of Amidon Elementary School, I heard seven-year-old black boys taunt and ridicule a contemporary because his skin wasn't dark enough for their tastes, and when his father attempted to console his son the child snapped, "How would you like it if somebody called *you* white?" No, bleaching creams do not sell well any more, nor "conk jobs" to take the kinks out of hair, nor white assurances that black patience will eventually bring better days.

Nor are young blacks alone in their growing militancy. As reports on racial insurrections show, older blacks often follow the lead of youngsters at a certain point of civil disorder. Middle-aged black politicians are increasingly adopting the tough rhetoric of their white counterparts. A decade ago only the white Southern politician breathed racial defiance from the stump, or spoke in code words comforting to his racist constituency. Today almost everyone does—on both sides of the color line, and all across the nation.

White "liberals" who once marched and sang for black freedoms (even though they may have avoided sending their children to integrated public schools or lived in all-white neighborhoods) tend to feel betrayed and sorry for themselves now that a large part of the black community rejects them. All that integrated praying, hand-clapping, and hymn-singing of yesterday having failed to purify the national heart, the black man wants no more. At a rapid rate, I think, he has given up on even the hope of white America's accepting a truly honest and significant integration of black people. Now he calls for black separatism, black control of black destinies, black institutions for black people—for, in short, black power. And it scares us to death. We don't want to give it to him. Having refused to integrate, we offer a domestic white colonialism and reminders of how much progress the black man has known in recent years. Yes, the white liberal—Manhattan intellectual or Harvard academician—seems as bitter and resentful against the new black militancy (and has as little understanding of its causes) as the Southern redneck or the Midwestern suburbanite. I believe, simply, that we have backlashed and polarized across the racial board, black and white alike, and that nobody much is likely to change for the better very soon. Increasingly, the two races find it more difficult at all levels to socialize, to communicate, to establish a basic trust or understanding. "The shine boy has the dream," John Howard Griffin wrote almost a decade ago. The dream was denied. Now, hostilities are worn on the sleeve. There are brutal pressures in our two separate societies to conform to the majority tribal viewpoint: to choose sides, to make it clear where one stands—else one be marked down either as, in the one case, a nigger-lover, or, in the other, a white man's nigger. "There is a little racism in all of us," Ramsey Clark said to a group in Cambridge one night over drinks. More and more, it shows.

I do not go into the black ghetto any more to perform such mild do-goodisms as demonstrating to keep a playground open or teaching remedial reading to the disadvantaged young. I do not strike up many casual conversations with strange blacks these days, nor otherwise intrude, in the absence of a black friend to run interference. Though at a party I might give a stunning stray blonde her social opportunity, I do not approach her black counterpart for fear of being judged an ass-pinching "white hunter." Invited by one black man to crash a party given by another, I carefully inquire whether my presence might be offensive. I am a white man, you see, and increasingly I am judged by blacks as arbitrarily as I once judged them; while there may be more than a little justice in this, there is too much discomfort in it to court. So I have joined my countrymen in becoming more suspicious, more ingrown, more tribal, more cautious, more fearful. On nights when the ghettos swelter I sometimes hear a siren off in the distance, and more than once I have wondered if it is the final signal that certain old white racist chickens are coming home to roost on my personal doorstep.

# Epilogue

*New Notes of a Native Son*

The following column, written by my friend Roger Wilkins, former Assistant Attorney General in the Johnson Administration and now an executive with the Ford Foundation, was published in the Boston *Globe* and the Washington *Post* in early 1970. Because it so powerfully describes the feelings of a perceptive black man in the presence of white racism, I have received Roger Wilkins' permission to reprint it here.

When it was all over, a number of men had tears in their eyes, even more had lifted hearts and spirits, but a few were so dispirited that they went upstairs to get drunk. We had just heard the President and Vice-President of the United States in a unique piano duet—and to many Gridiron veterans, it was a moving show-stopper. To a few others, it was a depressing display of gross insensitivity and both conscious and unconscious racism—further proof that they and their hopes for their country are becoming more and more isolated from those places where America's heart and power seem to be moving.

The annual dinner of the Gridiron Club is the time when men can put on white ties and tails and forget the anxiety and loneliness that are central to the human condition and look at other men in white ties and tails and know that they have arrived or are still there.

The guests are generally grateful and gracious. But the event's importance is beyond the structures of graciousness because it shows the most powerful elements of the nation's daily press and all elements of the nation's government locked in a symbolic embrace. The rich and the powerful in jest tell many truths about themselves and about their country. I don't feel very gracious about what they told me.

Some weeks ago, to my surprise and delight, a friend—a sensitive man of honor—with a little half-apology about the required costume, invited me to attend the dinner.

The first impression was stunning: almost every passing face was a familiar one. Some had names that were household words. Some merely made up a montage of the familiar faces and bearings of our times. There were Richard Helms and Walter Mondale and Henry Kissinger and George McGovern and Joel Broyhill and Tom Wicker and William Westmoreland and John Mitchell and Tom Clark (ironically placed, by some pixie no doubt, next to each other on the dais) and Robert Finch and Ralph Nader, and of course, the President of the United States.

One thing quickly became clear about those faces. Apart from Walter Washington—who, I suppose, as Mayor had to be invited—mine was the only face in a crowd of some 500 that was not white. There were no Indians, there were no Asians, there were no Puerto Ricans, there were no Mexican-Americans. There were just the Mayor and me. Incredibly, I sensed that there were few in the room who thought that anything was missing.

There is something about an atmosphere like that that is hard to define, but excruciatingly easy for a black man to feel. It is the heavy, almost tangible, clearly visible, broad assumption that in places where it counts, America is a white country. I was an American citizen sitting in a banquet room in a hotel which I had visited many times. (My last occasion for a visit to that hotel was the farewell party for the white staff director and the black deputy staff director of the United States Commission on Civil Rights.) This night in that room, less than three miles from my home in the nation's capital, a sixty-per-cent black city, I felt out of place in America.

This is not to say that there were not kind men, good men, warm men in and around and about the party, nor is it to say that anyone was personally rude to me. There were some old friends and some new acquaintances whom I was genuinely glad to see. Ed Muskie, who had given a very funny and exquisitely partisan speech (the Republicans have three problems: the war, inflation, and what to say on Lincoln's Birthday), was one of those. I was even warmly embraced by the Deputy Attorney General, Mr. Kleindienst, and had a long

conversation with the associate director of the FBI, Mr. De-
Loach.

But it was not the people who so much shaped the evening. It was the humor amidst that pervasive whiteness about
what was going on in the country these days that gave the
evening its form and substance. There were many jokes
about the "Southern strategy." White people have funny
senses of humor. Some of them found something to laugh
about in the Southern strategy. Black people don't think it's
funny at all. That strategy hits men where they live—in their
hopes for themselves and their dreams for their children. We
find it sinister and frightening. And let it not be said that the
Gridiron Club and its guests are not discriminating about
their humor. There was a real sensitivity about the inappro-
priateness of poking fun that night at an ailing former President, but none about laughing about policies which crush the
aspirations of millions of citizens of this nation. An instructive
distinction, I thought.

There was a joke about the amendments to the Constitution (so what if we rescind the First Amendment, there'll
still be twenty-five left), and about repression (you stop bugging me, I'll stop bugging you), and there were warm, almost
admiring jokes about the lady who despises "liberal Communists" and thinks something like the Russian Revolution occurred in Washington on November 15th.* There was
applause—explosive and prolonged—for Judges Clement
Haynsworth and Julius Hoffman (the largest hands of the
evening by my reckoning).

As I looked, listened, and saw the faces of those judges
and of the generals and of the admirals and of the old members of the oligarchies of the House and Senate, I thought of
the soft, almost beatific smile of Cesar Chavez, the serious
troubled face of Vine Deloria, Jr., and the handsome, sensitive faces of Andy Young and Julian Bond of Georgia. All
those men and more have fought with surely as much ideal-
ism as any general ever carried with him to Saigon, with as
much courage as any senator ever took with him on a fact-

---

* Moratorium Day, protesting the Vietnam War.

finding trip to a Vietnam battlefield, or even as much hope, spirit, and belief in the American dream as any Peace Corps kid ever took to the Andes in Peru. But the men I have named fought for American freedom on American soil. And they were not there. But Julius Hoffman was.

As the jokes about the "Southern strategy" continued, I thought about the one-room segregated schoolhouse where I began my education in Kansas City. That was my neighborhood school. When they closed it, I was bused—without an apparent second thought—as a five-year-old kindergartener, across town to the black elementary school. It was called Crispus Attucks.

And I thought of the day I took my daughter when she was seven along the Freedom Trail in Boston, and of telling her about the black man named Crispus Attucks who was the first American to die in our revolution. And I remember telling her that white America would try very hard in thousands of conscious and unconscious ways both to make her feel that her people had no part in building America's greatness and to make her feel inferior. And I remember the profoundly moving and grateful look in her eyes and the wordless hug she gave me when I told her, "Don't you believe them, because they are lies." And I felt white America in that room in the Statler-Hilton telling me all those things that night, and I told myself, "Don't you believe them, because they are lies."

And when it came to the end, the President and the Vice-President of the United States, in an act which they had consciously worked up, put on a Mister Bones routine about the Southern strategy with the biggest boffs coming as the Vice-President affected a deep Southern accent. And then they played their duets—the President playing his songs, the Vice-President playing "Dixie," the whole thing climaxed by "God Bless America" and "Auld Lang Syne." The crowd ate it up. They roared. As they roared I thought that after our black decade of imploring, suing, marching, lobbying, singing, rebelling, praying, and dying we had come to this: a Vice-Presidential Dixie with the President as his straight man. In the serious and frivolous places of power—at the

end of that decade—America was still virtually lily white.
And most of the people in that room were reveling in it.
What, I wondered, would it take for them to understand that
men also come in colors other than white? Seeing and feeling
their blindness, I shuddered at the answers that came readily
to mind.

As we stood voluntarily, some more slowly than others,
when the two men began to play "God Bless America," I
couldn't help remembering Judy Collins (who could not sing
in Chicago *) singing "Where Have All the Flowers Gone?"

So later I joined Nick Kotz, author of *Let Them Eat
Promises,* and we drank down our dreams.

I don't believe that I have ever been blanketed in and suf-
focated by such racism and insensitivity since I was a sophomore in college and was the only black invited to a minstrel
spoof put on at a white fraternity house.

But then, they were only fraternity brothers, weren't they?

* At the 1968 Democratic National Convention.

# Notes of Appreciation

To Willie Morris, editor-in-chief of *Harper's Magazine,* who on a rainy, boozy, midnight another life ago, encouraged me to follow my heart in abandoning the conventional restrictions of politics for the freer uncertainties of writing—and whose munificent talents have since been available in the most fumbling hours.

To Sterling Lord, who somehow discovered (as a good literary agent should) how to make that new journey less perilous than it might have been.

To Alan Williams, editor of this book, for his gentlemanly patience, good advice, and pruning of my natural excesses.

To Rosemarie, of course, who fed the writing body, who comforted it when the words wouldn't come, who shouted at it when it became absolutely necessary to visit the typewriter once more.

And lastly—as always when a white man takes up his priorities—to Wally and Janis Terry, Percy and Mildred Ricks, Roger and Eve Wilkins, Moe Davenport, Valery Pinson, Bruce Jessup, Roosevelt Weaver, and Vernon Morgan, and to their parents, their children, and their children's children—for reasons they themselves will best understand.

—Larry L. King

Washington, D.C.
October 1, 1970